HOT FLASHES AND HIGHBALLS

A PARANORMAL COZY MYSTERY

MYSTIC ON THE ROCKS

LYNN M. STOUT

For Rashmi

WHAT'S HAPPENED SO FAR….

If you haven't read the Extra-Ordinary Midlife Mysteries series, or you just want a refresher, catch up here!

"Day drinking?"

"I don't think so."

"Day drugging?"

"I don't think that's how they say that."

"Well something is going on."

I couldn't disagree. Samantha and I were watching Tawny, our friend, roommate, and business partner. She strolled through the office as though looking for something. Normal enough. What was not normal was the large piece of bubble gum she was chomping on and the loud smacks and pops emitting from that very piece of gum every few seconds.

She finally stopped, stood with one hand on her hip, and blew a huge bubble. Then with her pointer finger, she popped the bubble, twirled her finger wrapping the gum around it, and stuck the entire mess back into her mouth.

"Gross," Sam muttered.

Tawny had recently moved to Michigan and was living with Sam and me in the house I inherited a few years ago. She was in her twenties, slim and healthy, and absolutely gorgeous. Samantha and I had been best friends for decades and after my husband passed away a few years ago, and then Sam had her own trauma with a boyfriend she was accused of murdering, we decided to live together in my huge old Queen Anne house in the Detroit suburbs. We both needed to get away.

Of course, Sam did not murder anyone and there was a very simple explanation. It was my house daemon in Charleston. Sam was completely innocent. Police ruled it self-defense. We ruled it daemon-defense. Sam changed her name and left it all behind her.

So it was in this gorgeous house that we transplanted our real estate business, of which Tawny was an integral part. Except now, something was terribly wrong with her.

"Hey, Tawny, are you okay?" I asked tentatively.

She completely ignored me and continued to blow bubbles and pop them with her finger.

"Tawny!" Sam yelled.

She slowly turned and looked at us, blinking quickly.

"Um? Are you talking to me?"

"Your name is Tawny isn't it?" Sam said. Obviously irritated by the spectacle.

"Um? No? It's not? Okay? I'm Sherri? I think. Where am I?" Her eyes began darting between us and the door.

Sam leaned in and whispered. "Why is she ending every sentence with a question?"

I shook my head and stood. My instincts were on full alert. Sam and I were between Tawny and the door, but the way her eyes were dancing around, it was pretty obvious she was thinking about making a run for it. While I didn't know exactly what was going on, I was darn certain we didn't need her out running around in the streets.

Holding my hands out, palms up, and moving slowly, I moved towards her. "Tawny, uh, Sherri. I think something has happened here. We are friends and you are safe here. Will you sit down and talk to us?"

Tears gathered quickly and one blink was all that was needed for them to begin trailing down her cheeks. She wiped them away, smearing her eyeliner and mascara. She looked like a tragic raccoon.

"No. I need to find my mom? I'm fine."

As anticipated, she made a move towards the door, but Sam jumped in front of her just in time. She simply held her arms out, and the young woman didn't hesitate to collapse into her chest sobbing. Poor Sam looked confused and incredibly uncomfortable. Nonetheless, she held tight to the young woman.

Sam, like me, was in her mid-fifties. Unlike me, she did not have children and had never been married. When Tawny first came into our lives, Sam was convinced she was after her job at the real estate office and their relationship was extremely fraught. But over the following year, and too many adventures to count, they had become very close and Sam, I think, came to think of Tawny as her own daughter.

It was obvious, some part of Tawny also felt that way.

"I need some air?" Her muffled statement came out as a question.

"Okay. Let's sit on the porch. Or we can go for a walk."

I shot Sam a look. Was that a good idea? What if she ran off? Sam would never be able to catch her.

She shook her head slightly as though she knew what I was thinking and told me in that small movement that she had it under control.

Even with everything else going on, I couldn't help but be proud of her. Sam was the only one in our group without any sort of intuition, or psychic ability. While Tawny and I went about our days seeing and talking to ghosts, including the ghost of my husband, and communicating with other-worldly entities, such as the daemon who protected her, Sam would participate with a look that alternated between slightly confused and completely terrified. But each time something strange happened, she rolled with it, being the best sport ever. Not that any of us would say that to her face.

The three of us moved onto the porch and stood in a tight circle.

"Okay. You said you want to find your mom. Where was the last place you saw her?"

Sam was being so calm. I was impressed because either our Tawny was having some sort of major breakdown or something supernatural was going on.

Sherri said she last saw her mother at their house, which was just around the corner. As she spoke, she became more animated and excited.

"I mean, I walked here, right? So it can't be far."

Sam said, "Okay, then. Let's go look. Show me your house."

Then she looked at me. "Okay? And maybe contact Orenda while we're gone." She winked. "I've got my phone. I'll call you soon."

I nodded. That was a great idea. Orenda was Tawny's actual mother. Maybe she could reach her telepathically and get some answers. Whatever was going on, if Tawny was still in there, Orenda would find her.

~

I glanced from the retreating figures of Sam and Sherri to a new presence that seemed to materialize from the shadows of our day. There, leaning casually against a car, was Devlin McCloud. My heart hitched – not from fear, but an all-too-familiar frustration.

"Devlin," I said, a cautious note in my voice as I approached. "This really isn't the best time."

He pushed off from his car, that infuriating smirk playing on his lips. "Now, now, Connie. Just checking in on my three favorite gals. How's Tawny? She looks a bit shaken up. Everything okay?"

The casualness of his tone, so at odds with the gravity of our situation, grated on me. I fought to keep my voice even, though my hands itched to wave him off. "Tawny's fine, and so are we. Your 'concern' isn't needed here, Devlin."

Devlin laughed as he opened his car door.

"All right darlin', you need to calm down. We'll talk later."

Did he just call me darlin? And no way he just told me to calm down. Oh, hell no. The country girl, the bad ass woman, and the post menopausal bitch who lived within me joined hands deep within my soul. I stared at Devlin.

And he stared back. Then he pulled at his shirt collar. Then he gasped for air. He shook his head back and forth fanning his face with his hand.

"Stop it, Connie," he choked out. "Seriously. What are you doing to me?"

I jolted out of the trance and almost said I was sorry. Thank goodness, I didn't. Screw that. I wasn't sorry. I wasn't even sure what happened, but either way, he was a little turd and whatever that was, was just fine with me. Even if only because he didn't like it.

I began to walk away then turned back and stared at him again. He hit the gas and I couldn't help a smug smile at the sound of his tires squealing.

My smile didn't last long though. Sam was calling.

"Connie, we have a problem."

"It's the house we were buying. Someone came in and tore it down. It's where Sherri used to live. It's bad, Connie. She won't stop crying. We're coming back right now."

I hung up and tried to think of the best way to handle this. I still needed to call Orenda, but something inside me said to wait and give this a little more thought.

Houses like that one were the reason our business existed. The entire area was speckled with old houses that were abandoned during Detroit's decline. Slowly but surely, the city and the surrounding areas were coming back to life. Literally and figuratively. Our company, CST, was proud to be playing a part in the revitalizing.

Sam and Tawny both had their Michigan licenses. Much like the agency we all worked for in Charleston, this one also specialized in houses that were haunted. Of course, we didn't advertise that way. Instead, we quietly went about our business buying old houses that were marked for blight removal. First, Tawny or I would go in and check if any ghosts or spirits were left there. We still weren't sure what would happen to them when a house was demolished, but we didn't want to take the chance. Especially with Devlin lurking around.

If there was a ghost, I would get to know them and assess their situation. Sometimes they needed help passing over, sometimes they wanted to stay where they were. If the latter was the case, and if the house could be saved, we bought it and began renovations. When it was to the point of being livable, we'd sell to one of a few people we trusted who would move in, live there for however long it took to completely renovate and put on the finishing touches. When they were ready to sell, we served as the agent, because, well, the houses were haunted.

This is where Tawny and Sam came in. One of them was always the selling realtor for the house flippers. The three of us were quite adept at sniffing out the unique buyers who just happened to be okay sharing their home with a ghost. In fact, oftentimes we had referrals from others in our circle, many coming from Madame, herself, who sought out our special houses.

All we had to do was get to them before Devlin did.

~

Devlin. Not only the reason we worked with such urgency, but also the reason my husband was gone.

Devlin McCloud believed he was on a mission to rid the world of any supernatural being. Once he discovered that we could see spirits and ghosts, he began following us all. He carried a small box with him that somehow trapped souls. This box was how I lost my husband, Joe, for the second time.

Joe had returned in his ghost form and over the year that I got to have him again, we'd fallen back in love. It was strange, but also wonderful. His strength grew exponentially as our relationship rekindled. But when Devlin trapped the spirit of Tawny's grandmother, Beezel, the daemon who had protected Sam that night, and then catnapped Lex, Joe had to step in. And he was in a unique position to do something that would save everyone. That's just the kind of guy he became during his second chance. He sacrificed himself for all of them, and that night a lot of souls found peace. I only hope his was one of them.

"Did I hear my name?" Lex sat in the doorway.

"What?"

"Did I hear you say my name? What are you doing?"

"Nothing. Thinking. Some stuff is going on and it got me to thinking about the last few years. Sit with me and I'll catch you up."

I was on the small couch in the sitting room and patted the seat next to me. Lex jumped up and sat beside me. His large green eyes were watching closely and his grey tail flicked back and forth.

“What’s going on, Connie? Remember, no more secrets.”

Lex sort of came with the house. He was placed here to monitor the previous owner and intercept her actions, should she become dangerous. Which she did. So he did. When she died, his job was complete, but he decided to stick around.

Lex and Beezel were best friends, and their connection is what ultimately brought Sam, Tawny and me to this very place. It was all very mystical and intricately planned amongst those on a private supernatural mind-reading channel that I had zero access to. It used to bother me that all these people were ‘talking’ about me, and I couldn’t hear what they were saying.

But knowing Tawny and Lex both loved me and would never allow any harm to come to me, I learned to accept it. I didn’t love that a talking cat, I mean, a talking daemon in the form of a cat, knew more about my life than I did, though.

Nonetheless, Lex came through for us all, many times. And he was a valuable member of our group. Loved and adored by Sam and me, and tolerated by Tawny who was not a cat person, he lived a sort of hybrid life somewhere between feral cat and refined human.

Also, he had a pet cat he named Snowball. She

was a bit over a year old and an actual, non talking, normal cat. Lex adopted her and acted like a father to the little fluffy, white thing.

He was still watching me closely with one eyebrow raised. He wasn't the most patient being. I began to fill him in on what was going on with Tawny.

"She and Sam are on their way back right now," I finished. Then I told him about Devlin being out front.

At that, Lex's tail bushed out like a very long, grey bottle brush and he arched his back and hissed. He was normally a very dignified daemon cat. He was a tuxedo grey so his white belly and chest looked like a shirt, while his grey back and tail reminded me of a formal tuxedo with tails. His paws were white, of course, gloves and boots. And the tiny little speck of white on his chin completed the assemble with a spiffy bow tie.

But seeing him now, all puffed out and hissy, I had to stifle a smile. He was so protective of us all and frequently lost his cool when he felt we were threatened.

I reached out and stroked his back.

"Thank you," he said, slowly relaxing. "That helps. How close are they? I want them in the house quickly, especially with Devlin the Dick poking around."

His phrasing made me choke back a laugh but

with perfect timing, the front door flew open. A worried Sam entered with a shivering Sherri under her protective arm.

And that's when I realized.

It's no longer my story.

Now, it's Samantha's turn...

CHAPTER 1

"Day drinking, maybe?"

"No, I don't think so."

"Day drugging?" I glanced at Connie to gauge her reaction.

"I don't think that's how they say it."

I rolled my eyes. Connie could be so serious sometimes. I know she's been through a lot, but still, lighten up. I wanted to say, of course, that's not how 'they' say it, and obviously, I was joking.

Instead, I said, "Well, whatever it is, something is definitely going on with her."

We sat at our desks in a room we'd turned into our office. Tawny and I were establishing our real estate business with a twist. The twist was the ghosts and other spirits that stayed long after they should have found peace. At least that's how Connie puts it.

She and Tawny talk to ghosts. They can see them and interact with them almost as easily as you and I sitting down to talk. It used to drive me crazy. Especially when Joe, Connie's husband, died a few years ago. He came back as a ghost and, oddly enough; I was the first one to accept that something mystical was happening, even though I was the only one who couldn't see him.

My attention turned back to Tawny. She wandered across the room with a huge pink glob of bubble gum bobbing from her pursed lips. Good grief, it was almost as big as her head. If it popped, she'd have it in her hair and all over her face.

Connie cleared her throat. "Hey Tawny, are you okay?"

She didn't reply. Only blew another bubble and popped it.

"Tawny?" Connie tried again.

Another pop. She chewed like a lazy cow chewing her cud. I'd about had it.

"Tawny!" I yelled. She turned her huge eyes on me.

"Are you talking to me?"

"Yes. That's your name. What is going on with you?"

She twirled her hair around her finger and looked around the room, acting as though she'd never been here before.

"Um? No? It's not? Okay? I'm Sherri? I think. Where am I?" Now that we had her attention, her eyes darted between us and the door. She acted like she might try to make a break for it.

It didn't take a genius to recognize that would be a terrible situation. No way she should be by herself, much less alone outside. In fact, she probably needed to go to the hospital.

I wondered if she was having a stroke.

Connie slowly moved out from behind her desk and began taking slow steps towards Tawny. She held her hands out, palms showing, as though trying to calm a wild animal.

"Tawny. Sherri? Something strange is going on here, but we are friends and you are safe. Will you sit down and talk to us?"

"No. I need to find my mom? I'm fine."

It was happening. She was about to make a run for the door, so I jumped in front of her at the last moment. She stopped short, her face twisted into anger, then crumpled into sobs. She collapsed into my arms, and I held her tight.

I'd never had children of my own. Connie's kids were my adopted family. They even called me Aunt Sam. By now, in my mid-fifties, I definitely would not be having children. It used to bother me, but after a year of her pestering me half to death, I've come to love Tawny. At twenty-six, she didn't need me to mother her, plus she had her own mom, so our relationship settled somewhere between older sister and mother, but definitely friends.

"I need some air?" She mumbled into my shoulder.

"Okay. Let's sit on the porch. Or we can go for a walk."

I felt Connie's eyes on me. I knew what she thought. She might as well have been holding a flashing neon sign above her head.

I sent her a look that I hoped conveyed my thoughts. *She won't run off. I've got her. Trust me.*

Connie smiled and nodded. It's like she could read my mind or something, which didn't surprise me. It only added to the list of her abilities. It seems like with every passing month, she managed to do something else magical and amazing.

The three of us moved onto the front porch and stood in a circle. We arranged Tawny with her back towards the house. She'd have to get past both of us if she tried to run again.

"Okay. You said you want to find your mom. Where was the last place you saw her?" I asked.

This was strange. Connie and I both knew Tawny's mother, Orenda. She lived in Charleston, our old home town. But this person wasn't talking about Orenda. This person, who looked like Tawny, but somehow wasn't, was talking about someone else.

She explained that the last time she saw her mother was at their house, a few blocks away. As she spoke, she became more animated and convinced this had to be the answer. Her family still lived a few streets away.

Connie and I locked eyes, both of us thinking the same thing. There was a house in the area scheduled to be demolished in a few days. We'd been trying to get into the house first so Connie and Tawny could check for ghostly inhabitants, but we kept running into roadblocks. It bothered them both a lot. Maybe Tawny found out something new and checked it out on her own. And then maybe, just maybe, Sherri was a terribly misplaced ghost.

There was only one way to find out.

"Okay, then. Let's go look. Connie, could you contact Orenda? I've got my phone. I'll call you soon."

"Definitely," she said. "Be careful, okay?" She said, already pulling her phone from her back pocket. Tawny and I descended the steps, turned left, and started down the sidewalk.

I glanced back when I heard Connie's voice, loud and insistent.

"Oh, hell no! Get out of here! This is not your business." She was charging down the sidewalk towards none other than Devlin McCloud.

Crap.

I needed to get as far away from him as possible. Connie could handle herself. I needed to protect Tawny... or Sherri.

I smelled the dust in the air before I saw the remains of the house. We were right. It was the one we thought, and they had demolished it ahead of schedule. This was the only time that has happened since we began this business. Usually, communities had to wait months, even years, to have dangerous and neglected houses demolished. Then it took even longer to clean up the lots before the neighborhoods could return to their former glory. It was beyond sad.

Sherri picked up her pace. She craned her neck, trying to glimpse the house. I knew she was looking for the tall spire that used to peek through the trees. As we grew closer, my fears were validated. Neither of us could see the tower or the steeped roof that had stood as long as it could. Age and neglect left them decaying and collapsing, but they'd been there, holding on. Now, nothing was left but a subtle shimmering cloud of pinkish dust.

I held her hand, and we gingerly approached what used to be Sherri's house. An enormous pile of terracotta bricks sat in the center of the lot. They had stacked dark grey pieces of slate in a corner. Piles of rubble, wood, and bricks littered the ground. They had thrown the sheets of plywood that used to cover the gaping windows to the side.

"It was here! Why isn't it here? Where's my house? Where's my mom?"

"I don't know, honey."

"What happened? Why is my house gone?"

She kept asking questions that neither of us knew the answers to.

"We'll figure it all out. I promise."

She nodded, keeping her eyes riveted to the remains of her childhood.

A bright spot of color from the yellow power shovel caught my eye. It paused in midair as though not quite finished, the sharp edges of the shovel poised for another bite. I'd watched enough of those things to know the process, and my stomach churned. I couldn't imagine what Sherri must have experienced when that giant, loud thing crashed through the walls of her home. She must have been terrified.

She was. That's why I let her in.

Great, now I was hearing things. The voice in my head sounded like Tawny, but neither Tawny, nor Sherri, had said anything. I pressed the palms of my hands into my eyes. They watered from all the dust and, if I'm honest, a few tears. The entire scene was heartbreakingly sad.

I gave her another minute, then gently took her hand.

"We should go back now. There's a lot for us to talk about and -,"

"I'm a ghost, aren't I?"

That caught me off guard.

Most ghosts, according to Connie and Tawny, struggled to understand what was happening to them. Often, it involved a lot of explaining and convincing before they would accept the hard truth. Obviously, Sherri had died young, so it was even more surprising how quickly she realized her situation.

I decided to treat her with respect and not lie or sugar-coat anything.

"Yes, you are."

"How did this happen to me?"

"I don't know. Yet. But I promise you, you are with the right people to get to the bottom of it all. And you are safe."

She nodded. "I know. Like, I believe all that. But it's pretty gnarly."

I stifled a smile and asked, "Do you know when you died? What year it was, or how old you were?"

"Yeah, I was, like, sixteen? And I think it was 1986. I don't remember how, though."

"That's sort of what I thought. Okay, let's get you home and see what we can figure out."

"Wait!"

She stopped me again.

"Yes?"

"Whose body is this? I mean, it's pretty awesome and I'm not about to wig out or anything, but, like, it's...,"

She swayed backwards on her heels. I wrapped an arm around her waist and we started walking. Tawny is young and fit, but I am old and...not. I didn't think I could carry her and, not knowing what was happening with Devlin back at the house, I didn't want to approach with any vulnerabilities.

Still, by the time we made it to the house, Sherri was close to fainting, and I was exhausted and worried.

Thankfully, there was no sign of Devlin and we quickly climbed the steps to the porch. I flung the door open, and Connie and Lex jumped up. Connie helped get Sherri settled on the sofa and I collapsed next to her.

"We have a lot to talk about," Connie and I said at the same time.

~

It didn't take long before Sherri fell asleep. She and Lex were spooning and we'd covered them both with a soft, fluffy blanket. We made Lex promise not to talk in order to give Sherri time to process all that had already happened.

The addition of a talking daemon cat would certainly have been too much. For now, Lex simply tried to purr. Tried, because he really couldn't. He sounded like a lawn mower that refused to completely start and instead sputtered and choked. Still, the noise he made was consistent and calming in a strange way.

Connie and I talked in lowered voices. We knew Sherri was listening in that state between awake and asleep, where you hear what's happening, but you don't care enough to participate.

With two large glasses and a bottle of St. Julian Late Harvest Riesling, Connie and I sat on the other sofa.

"You start," we both said at the same time.

We laughed and clinked glasses.

"You first. Mine is going to take longer," I said.

Connie nodded. "Okay, so Devlin showed up out front after you left. I'm pretty sure he's been lurking around. I yelled at him and walked up to the car. Then, in his stupid, annoying, makes me want to stab his eyes out accent, he says, 'Now, now, Connie. I'm not here to cause trouble. I just wanted to check in on my three favorite gals. See how y'all are doing. Tawny seems a little shaken. She feeling okaaaay?'"

I laughed at Connie's impersonation of his accent. She did it perfectly, drawing out each syllable, especially the last one.

"I told him she's fine, and that nothing is wrong and he needed to go away. Then I reminded him we were most definitely not his 'gals'. What a creep."

I agreed with her, but before I spoke, she was flapping her hands.

"Oh, oh and get this! He called me 'darlin' and told me to 'calm down'!"

Oh, no. There's no way that went well. I can only imagine what it was like for her to hear Devlin's condescending words. Seriously? Telling her to 'calm down'?

As though reading my mind, she continued.

"Yeah, exactly what you're thinking. All this anger and heat inside me boiled over. Like a hot flash on steroids or something. It's like I got a superpower."

I laughed at the idea of menopausal super heroes, but Connie remained serious.

"The thing is, I think there's something to it. Devlin started to sweat. Then he was gasping for air, tearing at his shirt collar and turning red as a beet. He begged me to stop and said he couldn't breathe. I didn't know what he was talking about, so I ended up walking away. I do not know what I did or how I did it."

She sat back and sighed.

Great. So there's another supernatural ability for Connie. I was happy for her. No, really. Happy.

CHAPTER 2

"What did you find out about Tawny or Sherri?"

Connie watched me closely as she refilled our glasses. I was still thinking about her new abilities to, what would you call it, Darth Vader someone? Her question snapped me back.

I explained it was indeed the house that we thought it was and that it was now demolished.

"They weren't supposed to do that for another week."

"I know. Something must have changed. Maybe Tawny knew something we didn't. Maybe she went to stop it or to sneak in before it happened. Then, somehow, Sherri ended up with her. It was definitely Sherri's house."

We spent the next several minutes discussing her predicament.

"So, she knows that she's a ghost, and she took it really well. She knows she died in 1986, when she was sixteen. Oh, and she came right out and told me she knows she's in Tawny's body."

"Wow. So young. She would be about our age now if, you know..."

She was right. I hadn't thought of that. We were sixteen and seventeen in 1986.

"Do we know how?" She asked.

I shook my head. "She doesn't remember."

We sat in silence for several minutes, both of us lost in our thoughts. I was thinking about all the experiences I'd had over the past decades while Sherri was locked away in her old house, probably alone, as it decayed and crumbled around her. She must have been so lonely, so scared.

She was. That's why I let her in. Like I said before.

There was that voice again. I looked around the room for the source. Sherri and Lex slept deeply now, gently breathing in sync. Connie held her wine glass in front of her and stared into the middle distance. Her eyes glazed over slightly. She was thinking about her own life, too, and realizing what Sherri missed.

So where did the voice come from?

It's me. You're being kind of dense, you know?

So now the voice in my head is insulting me.

I took a long sip of wine. Okay, fine. I'll play along. I closed my eyes and cleared my mind. I wasn't sure where to focus my attention, so I didn't focus anywhere. Suddenly, a series of images and thoughts flew across my mental landscape.

I saw Connie reliving her wedding day. I saw Sherri with a Walkman in a record store holding a Madonna cassette. I saw Lex sitting on the kitchen table, a tiny mouse dangling from his mouth. I saw...ew, wait! Has Lex been on the table with a mouse?

The image distracted me, and the visions disappeared. Shoot. I'm pretty sure I was onto something there. Was I seeing what each person was thinking about? Or was I imagining it? No, there had to be more to it. I wouldn't have imagined Lex with a mouse by choice.

I would ask him about that when he woke up. For now, though, I said, "Hey, Connie. What were you thinking about?"

"My wedding day. Sort of reliving the memories, you know? It's so sad, all the things Sherri missed. I feel like I need to be super grateful."

I agreed with her. We grew silent again.

Well, that explains at least a little bit. Maybe I could see images of what others were thinking about. But then again, Connie and I were so close, of course, I would have a sense of her thoughts during a stressful time.

The real test would be Sherri and Lex. What are they dreaming about?

Some of this was making sense, but I still didn't know about the voice. Who was talking to me? And how?

(And, yes, I know what you're thinking. The voice is Tawny. I know that, I'm just not ready to admit it.)

~

Today was worse. Somehow, Sherri found a few pieces of clothing Tawny never would have been caught dead in. Which, I realize, is probably not the best way to say that, all things considered.

Her hair was pulled into a side ponytail with what can only be described as an antique scrunchy holding it in place. She had access to the makeup in Tawny's room, and had applied it with alarming boldness.

She noticed me staring.

"What? Too much eyeliner, right? My mom always said that."

Her face crumbled when she mentioned her mom. We had to remember she was still a teenager. Only sixteen and feeling all the feels that come with that age, missing her family, and of course, being dead.

"No, you look great," I smiled. "Come sit down. We need to talk and get some things figured out."

She leaned against the doorway, arms crossed

over her chest and head down. "Do we have to? I don't wanna talk. I don't know anything. Let's just chill out, okay?"

I bit my tongue because no, we wouldn't be 'chilling out' today. I remembered that attitude when Connie's kids went through their teen years. I had to explain to Sherri that we didn't have time for that and she didn't have a choice. If we were going to get to the bottom of all of this and figure out what was going on, she would have to suck it up and try to remember some things. We needed to make a plan.

Before I could say any of that, Connie swooped in and hugged us both.

"Good morning! How did you sleep?" She asked as she poured her first cup of coffee.

"Pretty well, considering."

"Um, yeah, me too," Sherri mumbled, still leaning on the wall, arms crossed over her chest.

"You guys want anything while I'm up?" Connie pulled out a chair and angled the seat towards Sherri, who immediately shuffled to the table and flopped down.

"No, I'm good." Then she added, "Thank you."

I watched the scene play out. She'd gotten a mildly surly teenager to do something she didn't want to do, and she made her think it was her idea. What was this strange magic?

Connie picked up her coffee and joined us at

the table. She smiled at Sherri and then at me. She looked around the room as though seeing it for the first time. I observed the show with quiet curiosity. I didn't want to interrupt.

After a few moments of silence, the teenager couldn't take it any longer and spoke.

"I wish I could remember stuff, you know? It's like a big empty spot in my brain. I got my driver's license, then I drove home with my mom. We went into the house and then... that's where, like, everything just disappears."

Connie nodded as she spoke. In a slightly bored tone, she said, "Huh. Okay. I wonder if there's anything else?"

Sherri shook her head slowly. "I mostly remember wandering around the house. I knew my parents weren't there, but it didn't bother me. I guess I figured they were out to dinner or something?"

I could picture it easily. A young woman, wandering through the large house, alone. Watching helplessly as strangers came and went, furniture disappeared, the power went out and it grew darker. As walls and ceilings cracked and chipped, plaster and moulding fell to the floor. Leaks in the roof sending rivets of water dripping through the floors.

It was even worse than that.

Again, that voice.

I shook my head and tried to focus on what Connie was saying.

"Last night, I did a little research trying to figure out what might have happened to you. The eighties were a really rough time in Detroit. They had a lot of murders. Quite a few teenagers were killed."

Sherri nodded. "I know. But we didn't live in Detroit. We lived here. Whatdoyacallit? A suburb, right? We didn't have the gang stuff like in New York or Los Angeles. It wasn't that bad."

A thought occurred to me. "Sherri, do you remember what your parents did for a living? Where they worked?"

Sherri scrunched up Tawny's face and stared at the ceiling. Then she closed her eyes and rubbed them. She smeared a bit of eyeliner around her lids, making her look like a very tragic raccoon.

She began to speak, slowly at first. "My dad was a cop. But he was a big deal. I don't remember exactly why, but he was in the papers. I remember them saying the words 'task force' a lot. Whatever that means." Then her head shot up, and she looked at Connie. "Do you have newspapers from then? Can I see them?"

"No. Why would you think that?"

"You said you did research. Do you have, like, a microfiche machine or something?"

We both stifled a smile. Of course, she knew little about this decade, or the ones in between.

"Something like that," Connie answered as she flicked her eyes towards me and smiled.

"We'll show you some things later today," I added. "What about your mom? Did she work? And where did you go to high school?"

Sherri said that her mother didn't work. She stayed at home and took care of the kids.

"Wait! The kids. So you have siblings?"

That took her by surprise, and she hesitated before smiling. "Yes, I have a brother. Or I guess I had a brother. He was older than me."

"What's his name? Was he in the house with you?"

Sherri screamed and pushed her chair back from the table so quickly it tipped over with a loud crash. The noise startled everyone, but Lex reacted the most violently. He darted from beneath the table, feet and claws pumping to get purchase on the kitchen floor. Connie and I jumped up, knocking our chairs backward, hands over our hearts.

Then it became crystal clear. We were used to living with a talking cat. One who had absolutely no self control or sense of timing. One that did not think before he spoke. One that shouldn't have spoken at all.

"It...it...talked? Did it? Like, the cat? Is that a thing now?"

She held her stomach with one hand and pointed with a shaking finger in the direction Lex had run.

I reached for her hands and tried to make eye contact.

"Sherri, look at me."

She kept shaking her head back and forth.

"Sherri!"

Still, nothing. She was disassociating. Her eyeballs rolled back into her head and I grabbed her shoulders just as she collapsed.

~

We half carried, half dragged her to the couch and propped her up with pillows. She was awake, but barely cognizant.

"Do we need an ambulance?" Connie asked.

"Maybe. But what do we tell them?"

"Good point. Let's give her a few minutes."

I agreed and sat beside her.

"I'll get a blanket and something for nerves," Connie said. Then, as she wandered away, she mumbled to herself, "And we still need to see what she remembers about her brother, and for that matter, her mother and father. What happened to her family?"

Those were good questions, and I wondered about the answers as well. For now, though, I held Sherri's hand and stroked her arm.

That feels good.

That darn voice again. I was going to get to the bottom of it right now. No time like the present. Even when a million other things are going to hell in a handbasket, by all means, let's address the voices in your head, too.

You aren't hearing voices, Sam. It's me, it's Tawny.

I stared at the young woman before me. She looked like Tawny, but she was half asleep. Her lips didn't move at all.

"How am I hearing you?"

You're reading my mind, for lack of a better way to put it.

"Okay. Way to bury the lead."

I've been trying. This isn't easy. You aren't helping. You're stubborn.

Yup, that was Tawny.

"Okay. I'll ignore the fact that I'm reading your mind and deal with that later. For now, though, can you tell me what happened? Are you possessed? Are you okay?"

I'm fine. Really. And I'll try to explain everything. Will you stay quiet and concentrate? It helps me when you focus on only me. And when Sherri is quiet.

I opened my mouth to answer and Connie

bustled into the room carrying a small bag of THC gummies and a large pillow and blanket.

"I'm not sure that's a good idea," I said, nodding towards the gummies.

"I know. I'm not sure either, but Tawny loves these things."

"What about Sherri, though?" I asked.

"What are you talking about?" Sherri mumbled.

"It's THC gummies," I explained, then realized she probably didn't know what that was. "Like, weed, or pot, but in a chewy candy."

I heard two voices at the same time. One in my head and one a mumbled statement from the prone figure in front of me. They both said, "Give me one of those."

~

The gummies worked quickly. Tawny's body lay on the sofa, a soft smile on her face as she stroked Snowball's back.

"You don't talk, do you? You're a normal, sweet kitten, aren't you?" She cooed.

It was strange to see Tawny with a cat. She wasn't a huge fan of cats, and she and Lex had an understanding. She had no issue at all with the fact that he was a daemon. Instead, she was more bothered by the cat form he was in than that he was an actual talking daemon.

However, she was warming up to Snowball, Lex's adopted, um...child? I guess? Snowball was an ordinary kitten whose mother gave birth in our home, but Lex laid claim to the tiny, furry bundle and called himself the father. We soon realized it was best not to think about it too hard.

I hadn't told Connie yet that I could talk to Tawny telepathically. Mostly because I didn't fully understand it. I wasn't sure how I was doing it, or if it was really me. Maybe it was all Tawny, and I was messing it up.

Nope. It's you. Connie can't hear me.

Her eyes were closed and she absent-mindedly rubbed Snowball's head.

Lex really did a number on her. I tried to calm her down, but she was pretty upset. You guys need to explain him as soon as you can.

"Yeah, we will," I said.

"We will what?" Connie asked.

"Um, we need to explain to Sherri about Lex."

Connie gave me a side eye. "Well, yeah. Sure. Are you okay?"

OMG, please just tell her. This isn't a mystery or something. Own it so we can get on with this. I have a lot to tell you.

Wow, this was really Tawny in there. She didn't mince words.

Sherri eventually relaxed enough to doze.

The hand that was petting Snowball stopped moving and rested lightly on the kitty's back. They both were breathing deeply. Now I could hear Tawny clearly. This was a good time to find out as much as possible. But first, I had to accept what was going on and, according to Tawny, 'own it.'

I cleared my throat. "Well, this is new, but it seems I can hear Tawny. It's like she's in there, still," I pointed to her body. "And I hear her in my head. At first I thought it was my mind playing tricks, but now, I think I believe it."

"I knew something was going on! You can read my mind too, can't you?"

"I suppose so. But not intentionally. It's like I can see pictures of what you're thinking. And, now that I'm thinking about it, sometimes I can hear your thoughts when they are directed at me. I assumed it was because we know each other so well we can tell what the other is thinking. But, I don't know now."

I met her eyes and immediately an image of the sexy, young guy who mows our lawn, shirtless, appeared.

"You're doing that on purpose!"

She laughed. "But that proves it! And are you really complaining?"

"No, I'm not!"

"Can you hear Lex, too?"

That reminded me. "Yes, and we need to talk to him about bringing mice into the-"

You guys are hysterical, but can we please get back to my issue? I know it's not a big deal or anything...it's just me, lying around, being possessed!

"Tawny is getting upset," I grew serious. "She says she's possessed, although I think that's a bit of an exaggeration. But we need to find out what happened."

I couldn't hear my own words after saying she was exaggerating. Tawny's voice was loud and insistent.

LET'S PUT SOMEONE ELSE IN YOUR MIND AND THEN SEE IF YOU STILL THINK I'M EXAGGERATING!

I rubbed my temples. She was loud.

"Okay, then. What's our next step?" Connie asked as her eyes darted between me and Tawny's sleeping body. "I don't know who to look at," she added ruefully.

Tawny answered immediately, and I obediently relayed the information to Connie.

"She's not sure what's next. She says she was out for a run early yesterday and, on a hunch, ran by the house. She had a bad feeling."

Tawny explained that by the time she got there, almost two-thirds of the house was demolished. She was obviously upset and had her phone out to make some calls, but she heard someone crying.

So she snuck around and followed the sound, eventually discovering Sherri's ghost.

"Oh my," Connie sighed.

Tawny continued, and I relayed her words exactly as she put them into my mind.

"I could hardly see her. She was fading quickly and was panicking. I could tell she was just a kid. And I know we aren't supposed to allow them to attach, but what else could I have done? I had to help. I let her tag along, I guess."

"You did the right thing," Connie said. "I think either of us would have done the same."

"Yeah, it's okay. We can help her." I added. Then to Connie, "In the meantime, Tawny says it's easier for her to talk when her body and mind are relaxed." I paused and listened for a few moments. "She says Sherri doesn't fight her or try to quiet her, but she is still scared and uncertain. Better to do this when she's asleep, at least for now."

"Makes sense," Connie mumbled.

"Oh, and she said to make sure Lex doesn't talk again. She says she's too young to have a heart attack."

CHAPTER 3

When Sherri finally awoke a few hours later, Connie asked if she was willing to go back to the house.

"I've been thinking we need to go back to where it all started. Maybe it will trigger a memory or something that could help us. We need to figure out why the house was destroyed in the first place. And we need to know what happened to you and your family. If you're up for it, that is," she added gently. "Maybe you can direct us to anything that hasn't been destroyed?"

"Sure, I'll do my best," Sherri said. "But it's pretty bad there. I don't think this body would be safe in some areas. I don't want her to get hurt."

Well, that was adorable. Tawny was protecting Sherri's soul, and Sherri was protecting Tawny's body. Connie and I shared a mutual, but silent, "awww" moment.

With perfect timing, Lex crept into the room and did a figure eight around my legs. Sherri watched him closely as he did his best to appear innocent and harmless.

He looked up at us. "Me-ow," he deadpanned, drawing out the two syllables way more than was necessary.

"Lex...," I cautioned him.

He sat on the floor in front of Sherri and grinned.

"Good grief, Lex. You aren't helping! Sherri, are you okay?" Connie waved her hand at Lex as though to shoo him away. He stayed put.

"Yeah. I mean, like, it's weird, but you know, I'm a ghost and all, so what can I really say about a talking cat?" Sherri had a point.

I heard Lex's thoughts clearly asking if he had permission to talk now, and I shared this with Sherri, but not in those exact words.

"If he were to speak right now, would you be okay with it?"

"And it's okay if not," Connie added. "It took me a while to get used to it myself."

Sherri looked at Lex and sighed heavily. "Yeah, go ahead. Talk."

The fur on his back bristled. "I'm not an animal. You don't need to order me around."

“Sorry?” Sherri said. “I didn’t mean it that way.” Her wide eyes darted between Connie and me.

“No worries.” His entire demeanor changed. “I’ll go with you to the house. I can get into places that you can’t.”

And with that announcement, the ghost who was possessing Tawny made peace with the talking cat she’d just met. This day simply could not get any weirder.

We walked towards the house as Lex darted in and out of bushes, chasing birds and squirrels. For a daemon determined to not be referred to as a cat, he sure acted like a cat.

Sherri told us she remembered nothing about her family or what might have happened to them.

“All I remember is being alone in the house. At first, I thought everyone was out doing something, but eventually, I realized they weren’t coming back. I remember being confused and scared and then, over time, I sort of gave up and was, I mean, kinda just there. You know? Time passed, I guess, and I was just ... there.”

“We’ll see what we can find out about your family when we get back home,” I suggested. A simple online search would probably answer a lot of questions. “For now, how do we want to proceed?”

Lex had been listening. Without a word, he walked away.

"Lex?" I said, trying to get his attention.

He sent a message that only I heard.

I'm going to climb around the rubble. I'll stay in touch.

I told the other two what he "said" to me and we decided to wait where we were until we heard from him again. Sherri wandered around a bit, kicking at pieces of rubble with the toe of her shoe, while Connie and I talked in low voices about her tragic situation. We were determined to help her find peace.

After a few minutes, I heard Lex again. He was under most of the rubble in what he said looked like the basement. As he climbed down, he discovered markings and symbols carved into the foundation.

I shared what I knew.

“Okay, he says there are symbols on the walls. They look like they were carved by hand, and they're hard to make out because they're so old. He’s still looking around.”

“Can you describe them to us, um, Lex?” Sherri asked, her voice barely above a whisper.

She tried so hard to become comfortable with Lex talking out loud. I appreciated her efforts. I was still working on hearing him, and everyone else for that matter, in my mind. This was turning into a really exhausting day.

Still, I interpreted and told him what she asked. The response came back clear as a bell.

"He says they look like some kind of magical symbols. He says he doesn't know what they mean, but they look familiar."

We were all lost in thought wondering what these symbols possibly meant. Could they have something to do with whatever happened to Sherri's family. Were we dealing with a curse of some sort?

I sent Lex a message asking if he would be able to recreate the symbols.

He promised he would commit them to memory and show us when we got home. I told him to come out and reminded him to be careful. He was important to us.

I felt more than heard his expression of gratitude and love and it made my heart warm. But the feeling was a short-lived because almost immediately, something caught my eye. A shadowy figure stood across the street trying and failing to blend into the bushes. I squinted, trying to make out who it could be. Then it hit me.

"Guys," I whispered. "We're not alone."

I motioned with my eyes, and Connie and

Sherri turned in time to see Devlin McCloud step from the shadows. He waved his hat in the air.

"What are you doing here?" Connie called out. "Stop following us."

The man's lips curled into a smirk. "The question is, what are you girls doing here?" His voice dripped with arrogance.

"None of your business, Devlin. Go away." I hoped I sounded braver than I felt.

Instead of leaving, he sauntered across the street, his eyes never leaving Tawny.

"What's going on with the pretty young one?" He asked, his nose wrinkling and twitching.

"Gross," Sherri said, stepping back. "Are you smelling me?"

In one swift move, I stepped between Devlin and Sherri, while Connie took her hand and began leading her away. Devlin tried to see around me, craning his neck and dodging back and forth trying to keep his eyes on Sherri, but I ducked and bobbed right along with him and kept my body so it blocked his view.

He finally gave up. "Fine. I know something is going on with you gals. There always is, and I'll get to the bottom of it later."

He took a few steps away and just as I started to breathe a bit easier, he turned back and did a very poor Peter Faulk as Columbo impression.

“Oh! There’s just one more thing,” he said, with a very non-Columbo smirk. “You'll want to keep a close eye on your girl. There’s something going on here, and I know she’s connected to it. As usual, you gals are in over your heads, I do believe.”

I replied with a stunning display of intellectual acuity. “Yeah, well, whatever.”

He laughed and sauntered off back down the street, mumbling to himself.

Connie and Sherri reappeared. They had stayed close and watched and listened to everything.

“What was that about?” Sherri asked. “Who is that guy?”

“It’s a long story,” I said. “We'll explain later. For now, though, stay as far away from him as you can. He's dangerous.”

“Where's Lex?” Connie asked.

“Hold on.” I concentrated and reached out to Lex.

When I opened my eyes, Connie was smiling at me.

“You're getting pretty good at that,” she said.

“Yeah, well. We'll see. Lex said he’s towards the back left corner of the house. He found something and is dragging it out. He needs help.”

We crowded around the kitchen table, an empty bottle of wine in the middle and full glasses in front of each of us. Sherri was over the moon to be allowed to drink. We had quite the debate with the irony not lost on us. It was only yesterday we'd given her THC and then, not twenty-four hours later, we struggled with whether to allow her wine.

She was under age when she died, but her spirit was our age. Added to that, the body she occupied was twenty-six. It didn't appear we had much of an argument against it.

When Lex was under the house, he found a metal lockbox with a leather handle. It took several minutes of huffing and puffing before he dragged it out far enough that Sherri, in Tawny's small and fit body, easily crawled into the small space. She reached in and helped him move it the rest of the way. When we got it home, we broke the old, rusty lock and now huddled around what appeared to be a journal and some other keepsakes.

The journal was well-worn with brown and yellow stains on the edges of the pages. It was difficult to read the handwriting, but overall, the lockbox had kept the journal in fairly decent shape. We carefully inspected the items in the box, while Lex worked diligently on recreating the images he saw below the house.

Since his paws weren't made for using a pencil or pen, Connie arranged a large sheet of paper and a bowl of washable, nontoxic paint on the floor for him. He dipped his paw, and the tip of his tail, into the paint and painstakingly drew what he remembered seeing.

"I wish I had my hands," he mumbled under his breath.

No one heard him but me, and I asked what he meant.

Nothing. Forget it. Just concentrating.

"Listen to this," Connie said. "Today was the second worst day of my life. Today, we buried my daughter. The first worst day was the day she died."

She paused and looked up.

"That's my mom's journal," Sherri said. She rubbed her nose and sniffled. "Why was it under the house?"

"She might have stored it there and then forgotten about it. Look, we need to see if your family is still alive so we can find them. Hopefully, we can get some answers too."

"If they are alive, why did they leave the house?" Sherri asked. "Wouldn't they have sold it and there'd be someone else living there now?"

We explained to Sherri what happened when Detroit fell into bankruptcy. Issues with the auto industry cost many their livelihoods, and many homes were abandoned when their owners defaulted on their mortgage payments. There simply weren't enough jobs to go around. Then the people either left the state or moved away from Detroit, and the city's demise was in full swing. If that didn't happen to Sherri's family, it may have happened to the family who bought the house after them.

"Here, let's do a search and try to find out what happened to your parents." I opened my laptop and prepared to blow her mind yet again. "We can find out pretty much anything we want to know with this. Do you remember computers?"

Sherri nodded, her eyes bright and shining. "Yes, but they don't look like that!"

"They do now," I mumbled as I opened a browser window.

"Before you do that, take a look," Lex said. "I can't make any sense of what they mean, but this is about as close as I can get. Are these familiar, Sherri?"

"No, not really," she giggled a bit. "I'm talking to a cat."

Lex rolled his eyes and directed his question to Connie and me.

"Anything?" He asked.

We both shook our heads. The symbols definitely looked as though they meant something. We added them to our list of things to research. We were banking on the internet to answer a lot of questions.

~

Sherri watched with wide eyes as I searched online for any information about her home, her family, or even what happened to her.

Eventually, I found a few articles about her death. When I realized she had been murdered, I tried to close the laptop before she saw the headline, but I was too slow.

"Open that back up. Let me read it," she insisted.

She reached over my shoulder and silently pointed to a headline. I clicked the hyperlink and turned the screen so it faced her.

Connie read over her shoulder and mentioned useful tidbits.

"Sherri was sixteen. Suspicious circumstances. Left behind a brother, mother and father, grandparents. The family is encouraging anyone with information to contact the detectives."

"Tell me their names," I said, with a pen poised to take notes.

Connie spelled the detectives' names for me

and then added that it appeared the family moved out of the house, but there was no mention of where they moved.

"At least not in this article. I don't blame them. It would be impossible to live in that house after what happened." She put a hand on Sherri's shoulder. "Oh, honey. I'm so sorry."

"Can I see that?" She pointed to the journal.

Connie handed it to her, strategically opened to a page where her mother had written about Sherri and how special she was. It seemed to help lift her spirits.

She got to the end of the page and said, "Wow. Did she really feel that way?" Her finger trailed over what she'd read, pausing at random spots.

"Well, sure, honey. She was your mom. Both of your parents loved you. You were their child. Of course, that's how they felt. Didn't you know?"

"Yeah, I mean, like...I don't know?"

As they talked, I continued to scan the internet for more information. Unfortunately, I found something else that I didn't want to share. I kept it to myself for now and decided I'd show Connie later. It had already been so emotional for Sherri. I didn't want to add any more stress to her today.

Lex jumped up on the table and I had a flashback to the image of him sitting in that very spot with a mouse in his mouth. Before I could ask him about it, he waved his paint-covered tail towards the screen.

"What's this?" He asked.

"Careful! Don't get paint on my laptop, please." I tried again to close the screen, but Lex stopped me.

"It's an obituary for Sherri's father," he said. "Look."

"Thanks Lex. Yeah, I saw it, but let's dive into this later, okay? It's been a lot for one day."

Then I sent him a silent message.

Knock it off. He killed himself. She doesn't need to know that right now. Got it?

"So my dad died. And I guess my grandparents are dead, too. Gosh, the detectives maybe. Who else?"

Before we could answer her rhetorical question, Lex recovered. With a stroke of genius, he called for Snowball, who came bounding into the room and distracted everyone. Especially Sherri.

"Well done, Lex," I muttered.

He took a small bow as Sherri smiled for the first time that afternoon. She scooped the kitten into her arms and hugged her.

"I'm so tired. Can I take a nap? With Snowball?"

"Of course, you don't have to ask something like that. If you're tired, go to sleep. Do you want to stretch out on the couch? Or go to your room?"

"We'll be in my room. I want my bed."

~

Once Sherri was out of hearing range, Connie looked at me skeptically.

"Okay, what do you know? I can only assume it's bad."

I pulled her father's obituary to the front tab. After Connie read it, I pulled up another article that explained even more.

Police determined Sherri had died in a home invasion. While the article acknowledged they didn't know who committed the crime or why, they suspected her father was the actual target.

"I thought cops stuck by each other. Like family, you know? One of their own and all. I would have thought they'd want to get to the bottom of it and not stop until the creep was behind bars...or worse. What happened?"

I shook my head and hesitated. She still didn't know the worst part. Yet another article was linked and I pulled it up.

"Oh no! No, no, no!" Connie had only read the headline and her reaction was as I suspected. Sherri's father committed suicide shortly after her death. And it appears her mother and brother disappeared. Or at least didn't want to be found.

The writer of the article had tried to track them down, but without luck.

"I don't blame them for leaving," I said.

"Me, neither."

"Poor kid," Lex added. "We really have to help her."

Just then, Connie's phone rang. She answered and turned her back to us so she wouldn't be distracted. Lex and I continued to discuss Sherri's predicament.

"Maybe she can find peace and move on if we find her killer," Lex suggested. "That's how it works, right?"

"Sometimes, yeah. But remember Joe? He wasn't ready to move on and he hung around for over a year."

"But he had a purpose. Do you suppose Sherri has a purpose?"

"I don't know, Lex. We'll have to see."

"Well, that was interesting," Connie rejoined us. "That was Ted Canter. He wants to sell his restaurant."

"THE Ted Canter? The Overlook?" I asked, my stomach already sinking.

"Who is that? Do you know him?" Lex asked.

I met Connie's eyes, and we shared a mutual sigh. It's not like Lex followed the news. He had no reason to.

"He's currently standing trial for murder," Connie explained. "It's been in all the news reports. He killed someone at his restaurant and that's probably why he's trying to sell it so quickly. To pay his lawyers."

"Allegedly," I mumbled.

"What?"

"He allegedly killed someone. That's what the trial is for." I'll admit to being sensitive about this topic. I felt it was important to remind my friends that we were all innocent until proven guilty. "Remember my situation? I didn't actually do anything wrong, but still..."

"Right. Sorry," Connie added quickly. "You are absolutely correct. And that really makes us the perfect ones to help him."

"Yeah, like, maybe we can figure out if he's guilty or not on our own. You know," Lex winked.

"Or we could just take the listing and help the guy sell his business. Just do our normal jobs," I suggested as I reached for my laptop.

I saved all the other articles and opened a new window, prepared to do a search on this Ted Canter guy. Lex grumbled something about me not being fun.

"What was that?" I asked.

"Nothing. I didn't say anything. Me-ow." He did his best wide-eyed innocent look, but failed.

"Funny."

I began my search with the current local headlines. They accused Ted Canter of murdering one of his employees at the restaurant. It seems the victim was shot once, and they found Ted unconscious with the gun in his hand right next to the body.

"Ted says he does not know why he was there or what happened. And he says he's never shot a gun in his life."

"They have the body and the weapon. What's the motive? Does it say?" Connie asked.

"No. But that doesn't mean they haven't figured it out yet. Possibly it's not been released. Still, that's interesting. If he really did it, why was he there? What happened to him? What? Did he pass out? Was he knocked out?" I wondered aloud.

"Sounds like a setup," Lex said. "The guy is innocent. I can tell." His confidence was inspiring, but it had gotten us into hot water before. Thankfully, Connie came in as the voice of reason.

"Let's look into it a bit more, Lex, before we go breaking him out of jail or whatever. I agree it sounds suspicious and I wonder how the prosecution is framing their case. How they explain him being passed out and all."

"Either way, we have a restaurant to sell, so there's still that," I reminded my overenthusiastic friends. "Plus, we have a business partner and friend currently housing a wayward spirit. We already have a pretty big problem to solve. Let's focus on one murder mystery at a time, okay?"

"I wish we could start getting some answers instead of more and more questions," Connie said.

"Hey! I know someone who might help!" Lex exclaimed.

Then he winked slyly. We didn't need to be telepathic to know who he had in mind.

Madame!

CHAPTER 4

Connie, Sherri, and I drove down Woodward Avenue, dodging potholes and construction cones. We bumped our way to the circular drive of the large pink marble mansion. Years ago, it was converted into a restaurant and bar and, more importantly, Madame's downtown office space.

We'd been here before. Our first visit went poorly. We made a terrible impression on the majestic woman who ran the only conference geared towards ghosts, mediums, and telepaths.

Back then, we were new to the mystical world and bumbled around the conference the entire time, making jerks of ourselves. But Madame took pity on us and gathered us under her protective wing. Even now, I still don't think she likes me very much. Her first impression of me was as a skeptic who wasn't shy about letting everyone know how I felt about ghosts.

Madame had timed it perfectly, of course, and met us at the entrance with a wide-open door. She gestured to one man to park our car as she ushered us into the lobby of the building. Despite being repurposed, the old home remained opulent and lush. Colorful Tiffany glass filled the tall window casings. Rich walnut furnishings matched the majestic, winding staircase. Our feet sank into thick, rich red carpeting.

Madame smiled graciously as she took Sherri's arm.

"I'll call for you soon. You remember where to find me?" She asked. Without waiting for an answer, she led Sherri away down a heavily carpeted corridor.

Connie watched them and laughed.

"What's funny?"

"I wish you could see them," she said. "There's four handsome young men, or ghosts, I guess, circling her all the time. At first I thought they were there to help her, but honestly, I think it's eye candy. They're floating along after her like lost puppies."

"No!"

Connie nodded sagely. "How old do you guess she is?"

I thought about my answer. We knew she was

much older than she looked. In fact, a friend of ours, a spirit named Bert, died in the 1920s and he remembered her as an older woman even then. Regardless, she didn't look a day over sixty and I wasn't keen on being the one overheard trying to guess her actual age.

I answered Connie with a shrug. We made our way to the aptly named Ghost Bar and ordered Japanese whiskey highballs while we waited to be summoned.

"What does she already know about what's going on?" I asked.

"Everything," Connie said. "I mean, when I made the appointment I tried to tell her what we were coming here for, but she cut me off. She already knows everything."

"Well, that should make things easier, I guess."

Finally, a handsome young man, not a ghost, motioned to us from the end of the bar.

"She's ready for you now."

We took our drinks with us and followed him to her office. She and Sherri were already comfortable sitting like old friends on the sofa. Connie and I settled ourselves into overstuffed chairs. Immediately, two trays magically floated to our sides.

I couldn't see the ghost holding my tray, but by

this point, I'd been around long enough to know that's what this was.

I set my drink down and said, "Thank you," to the air next to me, hoping I at least directed my eyes and voice in the general direction.

Madame smiled. "Oh, my dear Samantha. You have come a long way, haven't you?"

I nodded and smiled. "Indeed."

She turned her gaze to Connie. "And my dear Connie. You lost your precious Joe all over again, didn't you? How are you doing, dear?"

Connie nodded solemnly. "I'm doing okay. It was the right thing, you know? He would have been miserable if he hadn't helped everyone like he did. And I trust that he's okay now. In a good place."

"I'm sure he is," she said with a wink. "But you are here for a different reason. Sherri and I have been talking, and I think I can help you."

"So Sherri told you? About Tawny and the house?"

"She didn't need to tell me, dear. I already knew, of course." She waved her hand dismissively. "I will tell you both, though, this young lady is stronger than you realize. She will be an incredible asset as you set about solving your mystery."

I assumed by 'mystery' she meant how we would find peace for Sherri and then get Tawny back, but Tawny's voice rang out in my head.

Nope, that's not all. We've got a straight up mystery to solve.

Madame interrupted my thoughts when she abruptly asked, "Where is your daemon?"

"Lex? He's at home. Why?"

Madame leaned forward, her eyes serious. "You must keep him close. He is your protection against evil, especially as you come closer to the truth."

"What truth?" I asked. "And what mystery?"

"I can answer this," Sherri said. "I was murdered. And when we figure out who did it, a lot of other stuff will make sense."

Silence hung in the air as we digested Sherri's words.

"What can we do?" Connie asked.

I motioned towards the floating tray, and my drink drifted within reach. I figured the way this conversation was going; I wanted it close.

"You must find her murderer," Madame said. "But it will not be easy. The symbols you found in the basement are a clue, but that is just the start."

"Great. So what's next?" I took a long sip of my whiskey highball and waited for an answer.

"You solve the crime. Then Sherri will find peace. Simple as that."

We sat silent, contemplating the implications of Madame's words. I somehow doubted it would be 'simple as that,' and hid my irritation. Madame was supposed to help us and instead, I felt more confused and frustrated than before.

"Thank you, Madame," Connie said. We all stood to leave, but Madame held my arm and asked me to stay.

Crap, she read my mind. I was in trouble.

"I'll meet you at the bar," I said, as Connie and Sherri left.

"You have new powers," she said simply.

My cheeks warmed, and I nodded. The last time Madame and I had spent any time together, I barely believed in the spirit world and I definitely had nothing of value to offer.

"Good for you. You will use them well."

"Thank you," I said simply. What else was there to say?

"And I have something for you." She handed me a piece of paper.

"What is this?" I asked.

"Something that will help with your confusion and frustration, I hope."

My face felt even hotter. Crap. She did read my mind. In an effort to stop my thoughts from screaming embarrassing things, I focused my attention on the paper in my hand. It was the address for the Overlook.

Why did she give me the address for a place we'd been hired to sell?

I looked up to ask, but she'd already left. I

found Connie and Sherri at the bar and grabbed a seat beside them. Connie met my eye, curiosity clear on her face, but I shook my head once and cut my eyes towards Sherri.

She got the message.

I really wanted another whiskey highball, but I was driving, so I abstained and had a glass of water while Connie finished her second drink.

We sipped our drinks and discussed our next steps.

"We need to go to the restaurant and get the contract in place," Connie said. "I don't think Tawny is in a position to do that, so this one is going to be all on you."

"Yeah, I agree. I'll set up an appointment for this afternoon. Do we all want to go?" I asked, looking at Sherri for confirmation.

"Yeah, sure. What else am I gonna do? I might as well tag along."

I didn't say anything about Madame giving me the address to the very place we already planned to go. I wanted to talk to Connie privately first.

CHAPTER 5

We had a few hours to kill before meeting Ted Canter at the restaurant and spent them doing a little more research. We gave Sherri a few more pointers on how to search online. Then she slouched into her chair, pulled on my noise canceling headphones and checked out.

I looked at my phone to see what music she was playing. She'd managed to find the Eighties on Eight channel with no guidance at all.

It amazed me how someone who was not a digital native, and who knew so much less than Connie or I did, could still navigate and adapt so quickly.

"Is it the age?" Connie asked. "Is that what makes it come so naturally?"

"I don't know. She is our age though, or would have been."

It's me. I'm helping her.

Ah, Tawny, of course. Then it struck me.

"Hey! You read my mind! Have you been doing that all along?"

My words startled Connie and Lex, but Sherri didn't budge.

"What?" Connie asked.

"Sorry. I was thinking and Tawny answered exactly what I was thinking about. She's reading *my* mind. Hold on, she's talking again."

Relax Sam. Not always. It's because Sherri is distracted and relaxed. And you're thinking really loud.

"Now?" Connie asked.

I nodded.

"We need you two to get better at this. Even if Sherri is awake and engaged, Tawny needs to communicate. Think about how useful that could be. Maybe with some practice. I mean, you can hear my thoughts, right? Even when there are other things going on."

I looked away and shook my head. I didn't want her believing I eavesdropped on her private thoughts. I knew I wasn't doing that, but how could ever convince her?

"I mean, of course you're not listening in all the time. I can sort of feel when you're there, but still...,"

"Good. I don't want you worried that I'm not

respecting your privacy. And I'm glad you can tell. So you know for sure."

Connie held my hand and squeezed. "I trust you."

I smiled at her and sighed. That was good to hear, especially after what happened the year before.

"Okay. Good. I'm glad. So, um, yeah, you're right about us working together more. Help me think this through. Sherri can't hear us at all, so Tawny can't hear us. But because Sherri is relaxed and distracted, Tawny says she can access my thoughts," I paused and Connie picked up the thread.

"She can access your thoughts only because of the strange situation. If it were just Tawny sitting there, she would be like me. Most likely she would 'feel' you," she wiggled her fingers in the air, "and know you were listening to her but not be able to listen to you. I agree that the communication thing now is because of the situation. Ask her." She jabbed her thumb in Tawny's direction.

"Okay, let me concentrate."

I hadn't actually tried to reach out like this before, so I really focused and Tawny came in loud and clear.

See? You think really loud.

Sorry, I tried to whisper my thoughts.

Then I told her what Connie suggested. *Is that right? Is that how you think this is working?*

Yes, I believe Connie is right. We can make this work. Sherri is a sweetheart. She is always thinking such nice things about you both and is really grateful to us all. She and I have been talking too.

"Really?" I said out loud.

"What? What did you find out?" Lex was getting involved now and rubbed his face on the corner of the laptop. Sherri reached out and scratched him behind the ear. Or did Tawny do that? This was getting confusing.

"Sherri and Tawny are communicating."

"That's wonderful!" Connie exclaimed. "It says a lot about how Sherri is handling all of this. And it really says a lot about Tawny. What a trooper."

Before I answered, Sherri removed her headphones, sat back, and sighed.

"So, my dad killed himself."

~

We all braced for the barrage of emotions, but they didn't come. In fact, Sherri was shockingly calm.

"It was probably because of what happened to me. One of these articles says he was supposed to be the target so I'll bet he felt guilty. Do you think he's still around here somewhere? Like a ghost? Maybe looking for me?"

I didn't need to be a mind-reader to know how badly all of us wanted to say that was the case, and of course, he was out there looking for her. But I don't think any of us really believed that. He'd have found her by now, right?

Instead, Connie, Lex, and I pretended a confidence none of us truly believed in and assured her that must be the case.

Sherri accepted our pathetic attempts with a wry smile. She knew we only wanted to make her happy. After a beat, she changed the subject.

"So, I wanted to tell you, well, Tawny, and I wanted to tell you some stuff."

She went on to explain much of what we'd been talking to Tawny about and how best to utilize my abilities.

"And I want you both to know, well, all three of you," she shot Lex a quick glance, "I am okay. I'm not freaking out anymore. What I want is to find out what happened to me and I want to get out of Tawny's body. She told me about your husband, Joe, right?" She looked at Connie, who nodded. "And he was attached to this awful taxidermy beaver thing. I'm not doing that, BTW, but she also said he got stronger and could exist on his own. I think I might like that."

"You mean stay here?" Connie asked.

"Well, yes, but only if you want me."

Connie and I rushed to her side and hugged

her. As she tried to fight us off, to no avail, she said through gasping laughter, "So it's okay?"

"It's more than okay!" I said.

"Tawny told me everything. So, whatever happens, I'm not scared. But I don't want to stay in her body any longer than I have to."

"We will get it figured out and you can stay here as long as you want," Connie gushed.

"We'll need to put a hold on that for now, though. We've got to get going if we're going to meet Ted on time. Everybody coming?" I looked at all the nodding faces around me.

"I wonder if they have any leftover fish?" Lex asked with a mischievous grin that turned into a genuine smile when Sherri spoke.

"Oh, Lex, you're silly."

~

Ted Canter owned The Overlook restaurant. The building used to be a private mansion and was a little over a hundred years old. It sat far back on the sprawling lawn from one of the busier roads in the area, hidden behind large, sprawling oak trees. A long paved drive wound through the trees and up a slight incline, providing a spectacular view of the house surrounded by rolling hills, a lush green lawn, and wide open blue sky.

A wide porch extended the length of the house

with tall ionic columns supporting the entryway to the Classical Revival style mansion. It was gorgeous, perfectly restored, and obviously well-loved.

I stood lost in the details of the beautiful building, remembering why I'd fallen in love with architecture in the first place. Connie interrupted my thoughts and brought me back to the present situation.

"Is it weird that I'm nervous?" she asked. "This guy might have done it, you know?"

"I get that. But it's not like he's going to hurt us. Right now? Right here? He has no reason."

As I slammed my car door, a grey blur caught the corner of my eye. I held Connie's gaze and nodded my head toward it. Lex was already on the prowl. He was supposed to be spying for us, listening in to conversations we couldn't hear. Instead, he appeared to be stalking a small group of geese along the pond.

"He knows about geese, right?" Sherri asked. "They are so mean and hateful."

"Yeah, he knows," I sighed. "But he doesn't care. He enjoys messing with them and getting them all riled up. Watch."

We paused on the top steps and watched as Lex dropped to his belly and crawled up behind one of the sleeping geese. The other geese were staring at him warily. Time stood still for a few seconds, then Lex sprang up onto his back legs, took two steps, and pounced on the unsuspecting goose. The entire flock went wild and began squawking and clapping their beaks at him. He dodged every one of them and darted through the middle of the flock. A few chased after him but gave up when he easily outran them. With a flick of his tail, he disappeared around the back of the restaurant, hopefully to do some work.

During the show, Ted Canter had come out and joined us on the porch.

"That's a new cat. I haven't seen him before. We feed the ferals around here, so I recognize quite a few of them. Word must have gotten out that we have the best leftovers in town. Hello, I'm Ted Canter."

He extended his hand, and we all shook as we introduced ourselves. Sherri seemed especially uncomfortable with the grownup gesture.

"Please come in and have a seat. Would you like anything to eat or drink? We have a few things available, although the kitchen isn't open yet. Tyler, come see if our guests want anything."

A surly young man, tall and thin, slunk towards our table. "You want anything?" He asked.

"Um," I looked at Connie.

"Uh, sure. How about some hot tea?"

"Yes, make that two, please," I added. "Sherri?"

"Coke, no ice." She said, avoiding eye contact.

That was strange. Then it hit me. Of course, sixteen-year-old Sherri found this scraggly man child to be attractive. She was that age, after all.

Tyler left without another word, ostensibly to gather our drinks, and we began talking to Ted.

"Thank you, ladies, for coming here. I do appreciate it. Things have been hard lately. Thankfully, business is still good, although there has been a slight drop-off. Apparently, people are willing to overlook a murderer if he's a good chef," he chuckled. Then quickly added, "I didn't do it. Of course, but it seems to be assumed that I did. You know how it goes."

The silence was a tad awkward as we tried to find something to say. Sherri continued to act bored and disinterested, but was not very discrete trying to sneak glances into the kitchen looking for Tyler, no doubt.

Connie finally piped up, "So, are you ready to put the building on the market now? Or are you thinking about it still, gathering information?"

"I'm in the planning stages, I suppose. It all depends on how the next court date goes. I'm out on bail right now and my attorneys believe our case is solid. I mean, they should, since I'm innocent and all. But you never know how these things will go, so I want to be prepared if I need to act quickly. How do you suggest I proceed?"

I stepped in at this point and Ted and I began

to crunch numbers while Connie excused herself. This was part of the plan.

When I told Connie that Madame had given me the address of the exact place we were already going to, she came to the same conclusions I did. There must be a connection. It would have been nice if Madame had come out and told us what the connection was, but maybe she didn't know. Or maybe she was being difficult. Either way, we were curious enough to figure it out for ourselves. That's probably what Madame wanted all along, anyway.

CHAPTER 6

Ted said he wanted a few minutes to look over the paperwork, so I caught up with Connie and we wandered through the main floor of the restaurant, pretending we knew what we were doing. We hoped to find some clues as to what actually happened here that night and maybe find out how the restaurant was connected to Sherri.

Turns out Connie also had a pressing personal issue that needed to be taken care of quickly before an accident occurred.

"Two children over twenty years ago and my bladder still hasn't recovered," she deadpanned.

I glanced back to the table where Ted was still thinking, his head bent over the paperwork. Sherri was twirling her hair, looking appropriately bored for her age. And the drinks still hadn't arrived.

“Let’s head to the kitchen and maybe there’ll be a bathroom on the way,” she suggested.

“And if we find Tyler, we can try to talk to him.”

As luck would have it, we found two doors, each marked with a sign that showed a man, a woman, and an alien. Connie chuckled quietly to herself and pushed the door open.

Suddenly, she was backing out and seemed very flustered.

“Oh! Excuse me!” She said.

I looked behind her but saw nothing. Connie said a man was sitting in the window seat of the enormous bathroom, staring through the window. He barely moved when she came in, as though he didn’t know she was there.

“He said to come back,” she whispered.

She opened the door again and carefully looked inside. I stood behind her.

“Hello?” She said. “Hi, I’m sorry. I didn’t realize anyone was in here.”

Her long silence told me everything I needed to know. She was talking to a ghost.

Eventually, she said, “Yes, I can. It’s a gift I have.” Then she asked, “Are you Franklin? Franklin Docker?”

Oh, my gosh! She was talking to the ghost of the man Ted Canter was accused of murdering.

Connie turned to me. “It is him! He’s asking me if he’s famous now.”

She turned back and spoke into what still appeared to me to be an empty room.

"Well, in a way, I guess. Do you know...what... uh, happened here?"

I knew this was the tricky part. Not all ghosts knew that's what they were right away. Sherri was a major exception, but then again, she'd had a long time to figure it out. Based on the news reports, Franklin Docker was killed roughly five months ago.

Connie said he nodded. "He knows he was shot and wants to know if that's why he's still here."

Feeling brave, I projected my voice in the general area Connie was facing. "We don't know, Franklin. They think it was Ted, though. Do you remember anything?"

She listened intently for several seconds, and then a look of relief washed over her face.

"He says it wasn't Ted! He said Ted is just as much a victim as he is and that after he was shot, he actually watched the killer knock Ted out and lay him down beside Franklin."

We were both pleased to have resolved the first part of the mystery and confirm that Ted Canter was indeed innocent. But now we had another ghost who needed closure. And somehow, both ghosts were tied to this place.

"Franklin, can you move around the restaurant? Or are you stuck in here?"

"Okay, good."

She paused, then added, "I understand. So you don't care for Tyler, huh? Any reason, beyond his bad attitude?"

Another pause, then she asked, "Who is Missy?"

Over her shoulder, she told me, "Missy is the dishwasher, but according to Franklin, she's a lot more than that. But Tyler treats her poorly, and it makes Franklin angry."

"Okay, let's go find Missy," I suggested.

"Yeah, okay, but first, uh, Franklin, could you? Um, do you mind? I actually came in here for a reason."

Connie smiled and shut the bathroom door.

~

Finally able to walk comfortably, and maybe even laugh or sneeze without incident, Connie looked a lot happier when she came out.

We took another peek into the dining area to check on Sherri and panicked.

She wasn't there.

"Oh, I hope she's not with Tyler," Connie said.

"Surely not. Tawny has more sense than that."

"Tawny does, but I'm not as sure about Sherri. Come on."

We hurried back the way we'd come and found

the kitchen. We both sighed when we saw Sherri there talking to another young woman. They were laughing, well, Sherri was laughing. The young woman was smiling.

"Hey Sherri," Connie approached them. "Who's your friend?"

"This is Missy. Missy, this is my friend Connie, and this is my other friend, Sam. They are nice."

Missy's eyes flicked upward quickly and then back down. She mumbled, "Hi."

Connie looked at Sherri for a sign of what we should do. It was obvious they were talking comfortably until she and I arrived. Neither of us wanted to interrupt, especially if Missy had any information that might help and she trusted Sherri enough to share it.

Sherri said, "I've asked Missy if she remembers anything from that night that might help us out. She said she was here, but she doesn't like to talk about it. She never spoke to the police, either. She just told them she didn't know anything, and they dropped it. But I think she could really be helpful...when she's ready, anyway." She gently patted Missy's arm.

"I'll help," Missy whispered.

"Thank you, Missy. That's wonderful. I don't think Ted did this awful thing. Do you?" I asked gently.

Missy shook her head.

"And we don't want him to be in trouble or go to jail. And we really don't want him to have to sell the restaurant. If there's anything you know that can help us-," Connie stopped mid sentence as Missy covered her ears with her hands.

But then we realized what was happening. Missy heard Tyler coming into the kitchen and was already protecting herself from his harsh words.

"Hey, idiot. Are you going to wash anything today?"

Missy blinked back tears as Sherri, Connie, and I stared at him, eyes bugging out and mouths hanging open.

Sherri recovered first. "Hey! You can't talk to her like that. What's wrong with you?"

Tyler shrugged her off and went about his business, completely ignoring her. Connie stepped in.

"You can't talk to anyone like that. This is a business. Does Ted let you get away with that?"

"No, I most certainly do not." Ted Canter had appeared in the kitchen just in time.

CHAPTER 7

He'd heard what Tyler said, and immediately Ted went into a rage. He stomped up to Tyler and pointed his finger in the young man's face.

"I've told you that you've had your last warning. If I ever hear you talking with disrespect to Missy, or to anyone, you are gone. That's it, Tyler. Get your stuff and get the hell out of my restaurant."

"Your restaurant? Good luck, old man. It'll be someone else's problem in no time. Just as soon as you're locked up forever. Freakin' murderer. You can't run this place without me."

"That's enough Tyler. Missy and I will be fine. Get out."

"Yeah, you and Missy. Right. Why do you even need her? You already have an actual dishwasher!

Why waste the money on her?" He pointed in her direction.

Ted moved quickly to put himself between Tyler and Missy and bellowed.

"We need her because I say we need her. I'm the owner. It's my decision. Now get out!"

We watched Tyler gather his things and stomp through the restaurant. We heard a crash and then the door slammed.

"He probably broke something. It's what he does," Ted sighed. He held his hand out in front of Missy. She laid her hand on top of his.

"Are you okay, sweetheart?" He asked gently.

Missy nodded. "I'm ready to work now."

"Okay, you do that. Let me know if you need anything, okay?"

She nodded again.

I noticed Connie looking across the room. She smiled and nodded her head as though someone else was talking to her. Fairly certain that it was Franklin, I made a mental note to remember to ask her what he said later.

I had to wait, though, because Ted still wanted to talk. He told us all about Missy with such pride. I wondered briefly if she was his daughter.

"She's absolutely brilliant, just has a hard time expressing it. I've tried so hard to get her more involved with the business side of things, but she told me in no uncertain terms that she was not interested. She enjoys washing dishes. I think the repetition and the quiet are appealing to her. Her mother told me she has autism. Are you familiar?"

Connie and I nodded, but Sherri said, "No."

We were ready to leave, but Ted launched into his own version of a literal Ted talk. He told us everything we'd ever want to know about autism and, specifically, how it affected Missy.

"Her mind is like a steel trap. No kidding. She remembers everything. I just wish she could remember something about that night that might help me. I hate to sound selfish, but, well, if I have to sell, that affects her too."

He made a good point. I was now even more curious to hear what Franklin was saying to Connie. I sensed her mind spinning wildly with excitement and anticipation. She was eager to spill the tea, as the kids say, and I was eager to...hear it? Drink it? Whatever.

Speaking of spilled tea. That's exactly what Tyler had smashed. We tiptoed across shards of broken teapot and cups as we made our way to the door.

I told Ted we'd speak again soon. I had some actual business to attend to regarding his potential sale.

When we got to our car, Lex was asleep beside the back tire where he couldn't be seen from the restaurant. I opened the door, and he woke up immediately at the sound. He hopped into the backseat and started talking.

The drive home was full of three people and a daemon cat, all talking over each other, vying to tell their story first.

Lex won.

He told us he heard things breaking and doors slamming, then saw Tyler storm out of the restaurant. He followed him and hid while he listened to his phone call.

"He stopped under that tree in the front. Of course, I couldn't hear what the other person was saying, but when he told them he got fired, I heard them yelling through the phone. Tyler, that's his name, right? Yeah, Tyler started apologizing and everything, but I think he was getting frustrated. He yelled something about finding someone else to do your spying and then hung up. I stayed hidden, and he got in his car and left. He seems like a real peach."

"Yeah, he's a gem, all right. I wonder who he was talking to, though. It's interesting he said that about finding someone else to do the spying," Connie said.

"Agreed. Someone had him planted there, but why? And they had to understand he would not find out anything major. I mean, we could tell just by the way Ted acted in those few hours that he'd never confide in Tyler. What information was he expected to get?"

Everyone nodded in agreement and then Connie told everyone else what and who we'd discovered, hiding in the bathroom.

"Franklin Docker, that's the victim, right? So now we know for sure that Ted didn't do it." Lex was excited.

I had to agree. It was so much easier to do business with someone when you knew they weren't a murderer.

"Honestly, after spending the afternoon with him, I was finding it really hard to believe he was dangerous. Unfortunately, Franklin doesn't remember who did the deed, though." Then I remembered Connie's conversation in the kitchen. "Were you talking to Franklin? Anything new?"

"Nope. He's as clueless as we are. He told me pretty much what Ted told us about Missy."

"Who?" Lex asked.

Connie explained to Lex who Missy is and what she means to the restaurant and, more importantly, to Ted.

"She probably knows more than she realizes or is comfortable saying, anyway. I really thought she would tell us something, but stupid Tyler interrupted. Hopefully, she will come around and at least talk to Ted," Connie explained.

"Wow, you guys. Do you think any of this has to do with me?" Sherri asked in a small voice.

I shot Connie a quick look, and she nodded once. It was time to tell Sherri what Madame had shared.

"So she gave you the address to the place that we just left? Even though we were already going there? Why?"

"It was her way of telling us these things are connected. Something about your life, how you died, is related to what's going on with Ted right now," I tried to explain, but I didn't understand it any better myself.

"Why would she be so vague? Like, why not simply come out and say something? What's her deal, anyway?" Sherri slunk down in the backseat, arms crossed over her chest, with her bottom lip sticking out. She was the epitome of the frustrated teenager and after her boring afternoon and after seeing how Tyler treated Missy, she had to be disappointed. We needed to do something fun with her.

"It's just how she is. We've learned to live with it," Connie explained.

"Hey, let's go to a movie. Does that sound like fun?" I changed the subject.

Sherri immediately perked up.

"What's playing? Gimme your cell phone and I'll call Moviefone. Is it still the same number?"

Connie and I hid our smiles, but Lex wasn't as discreet.

"No, you goober. Just Google it. Put in the theater. Or even search for 'movies playing near me.' Sheesh, even I know that!"

"Lex!" Connie and I chastised him at the same time.

We needn't have worried though. Sherri defended herself by gently tugging on Lex's tail and making a face at him.

"Lex, you want to sneak in with us?" Connie asked.

He declined. So we decided we would drop him off at the house, check movie times and then leave in plenty of time to grab something to eat and make it to the movie.

The mood in the car lifted considerably and then plunged again when we pulled into the driveway.

"What fresh hell is this?" Connie mumbled.

Devlin waited for us on the porch. He leaned against the railing as though he owned the place. Connie was livid. I stayed in the car with Sherri and Lex, fully prepared to drive them both away at the slightest sign that things were going poorly.

He'd already catnapped Lex once. I wasn't going to give him another chance to do that. And his interest in Sherri, although for him it was still Tawny, was unnerving to say the least.

I focused my energy on Connie and did my best to read her mind as she talked to Devlin.

At first, I picked up serious anger and a whole lot of words I would not repeat in front of Sherri. Then she grew quiet and listened. Her demeanor matched what I sensed from her thoughts.

In my mind, I heard her say, "I understand. I still don't trust you, but I appreciate you telling me this. Right."

I tried to communicate with her. What in the world was he telling her, and why would she change her mind so quickly?

I made my thoughts as focused and clear as possible.

Connie! What's going on?

And the response came right back to me.

It's okay. He's leaving. Let him pull out.

Excited by how well my telepathy worked, I fumbled around climbing over the center console and strained my back in the process. I was definitely too old for this kind of thing. My butt dropped onto the gearshift.

"Ouch! That's going to leave a bruise," I grumbled, to the delight of the crew in the backseat.

Eventually, I got settled in the driver's seat and moved the car out of the way so Devlin could leave. He waved as he drove by, but I ignored him.

By the time we all entered the house and locked the door behind us, Connie was already on the phone with Ted.

"Do you know a man named William Black?" She held a finger up and then turned her back to us.

"What's going on?" Lex asked.

"No idea. Give her a minute, though." Then I added, "Hey, Sherri. Look up some movies, okay? What do you want to see and what time? Let's be ready for when she's finished on the phone."

Sherri nodded and wandered into the kitchen, where the laptop still sat. Lex followed her, his tail bushed out and the fur on his back standing on end. The last few events obviously unsettled him, and I didn't blame him.

I sat and waited patiently. When Connie saw everyone had left the room except me, she sat beside me and put the call on speaker.

"Hey, Ted. You're on speaker now. Sam is here with me. Will you say all that again? I really want her to hear it from you."

"Yeah, sure. Hey there Sam, long time no talk," he laughed at his bad joke.

"Hey Ted. What's going on?"

"So your partner there asked me about a man named William Black. I really want to warn you ladies to stay as far away from him as you possibly can. He comes from a family that is well known in some parts as being heavily involved in the occult. It's the type of thing that's very dangerous."

I looked at Connie and mouthed 'occult' to her as I shrugged. I mean, technically, we were involved in the occult, too. That didn't make us evil people.

Connie nodded and put her finger to her lips and winked.

"Go on, Ted. Tell her the rest," she said out loud.

"Well, way back in the day, there were rumors about the Blacks. They were one of those families no one wanted to mess around with. They believed they should be able to get anything they wanted whenever they wanted it. And if they couldn't, if whoever had what they wanted didn't give it up, they'd try to buy it. If that didn't work, people started getting hurt. And I don't mean hurt like you're probably thinking. I'm guessing you know about the organized crime that existed around here back then, but I'm not talking about busted kneecaps and broken fingers. I'm talking about magic. Black magic. Evil curses. If someone from the Black family put a curse on you or yours, bad things happened one after another. It was worse than if you'd just died."

"What things, Ted? What would happen?"

"Your house might burn down. And then your car would be totaled. Your pets would die mysteriously. Your spouse would leave you, or get sick, or worse. And sometimes these things happened to the children. You would have the worst of the worst just keep happening to you."

I didn't hear anything else after that. My eyes snapped to Connie's. She was already watching me, waiting for my reaction. Was that the connection? Was Sherri one of the children whose family was cursed by the Blacks? Is this why she was still here? And why her father was so overwrought he could find no other solution besides the terrible one he chose?

"Okay, thank you Ted. We really appreciate your warning on that," Connie said.

"Oh, no problem. I really like you ladies and I want you to stay safe. By the way, how did you come to hear that name? He's not snooping around you, is he?"

"No, nothing like that. It came up in a conversation with an old friend. Thanks again. We'll be safe, I promise. And Sam will call you later with more information on the listing."

She hung up, and I asked, "I really hope you aren't referring to Devlin as 'an old friend,' although I suspect you are. He's the one who brought up William Black, isn't he?"

"Yup."

"Well, that's rich. One evil jerk warning us about another evil jerk. Like we would ever trust him. Right?"

Connie didn't reply, so I nudged my way into her mind and read her thoughts.

She did trust him!

"Connie! Why?"

"Because he was scared, Sam. I've never seen him so shaken. This guy is scary enough that Devlin was fearful, not only for himself, but for us, too."

We stayed silent for several seconds as that news slowly sunk in.

The sounds of Lex's nails stomping on the hardwood floors drew our attention. He hopped up on the couch between us.

"Well, someone's got you both upset. I can see on your faces. I can't imagine what that Devlin character had to say, but I know it wasn't good. Listen, though. Sherri needs this, so when she comes in here and tells you what she wants to do tonight, go with it, okay? And you both could probably use this too. Whatever this is, we'll get into it tomorrow. Let's take a break."

"What does she want to do?" I asked.

"Wait for it...," Lex said mysteriously.

With a few searches and the click of a "Buy and Watch Now" button, we were soon snuggled under a blanket with popcorn and ginger highballs, watching the only movie that made sense at that moment.

I smiled as the opening scenes of "Pretty in Pink" began to roll and Sherri squealed, "I love Molly Ringwald!"

By the time "If You Leave" played, Connie and Lex were asleep, Sherri was misty-eyed, and I was lost in thought.

CHAPTER 8

"Did you love it?" Lex asked Sherri the next morning. He was asking about the movie.

"Yeah, I really did. But mostly it was nice to be surrounded by people and do something normal? I think, you know, I miss being alive."

We all felt the gut punch when she said that. It was so easy to forget she was dead. And I know we all missed Tawny, too. This situation worked for now, but it wasn't a long-term solution by any means. We had to figure something out.

I tapped into Connie's thoughts, which completely echoed mine. I didn't hide it. She knew I was there and smiled. Lex was thinking the same thing, but his response was more aggressive.

"Get out of my head, you whackadoo!" He puffed up his tail and stalked from the room. I don't think he was truly angry, though. He laughed silently.

"What's our plan, then? We have to find a solution here. Sweetheart, you know we can't make you alive again. And earlier you said you would like to stay here with us. Of course, we'd love that, but we need a way for you to do it that doesn't involve Tawny." Connie said.

Sherri nodded. "I know, and I've been thinking about it and talking to Tawny. She told me all about Joe, your husband, and that horrible thing - a what? Like a stuffed beaver or something? And he was attached to it until he learned to move around on his own. I think that's kinda cool, but I definitely don't want to be, like, in something like that."

I laughed and explained to her that was simply the thing he ended up with. That didn't mean it would be the same thing she would have to use if she could attach to an object.

"It's called taxidermy, and it was his hobby for about a minute," Connie said. "His spirit attached to it right after he died. Maybe because he made it himself, or maybe just to mess with me since I hated it so much. But, yes, he eventually could move around almost as well as anyone living."

"Do you still have it, Connie?"

"Sadly, yes I do. Hold on a sec."

Within moments she returned lugging the two

foot tall, twenty pound, taxidermy beaver. Brodie the Beaver still wore his sunglasses and a Hawaiian shirt. He stood on a long plank of wood that served as his surfboard and added to the awkwardness of his entire existence. Without a doubt, it remained the ugliest and most appalling thing I've ever seen.

I was overcome with a sense of nostalgia, remembering all the times we'd taken that thing into haunted houses, carried it on airplanes, and traveled across the country with it in the backseat. It saw more crime scenes than I can count. I know Connie experienced the same reaction. Although her emotions were probably stronger as she remembered the times we'd had with the ghost of her dear husband. And, of course, the sacrifice he made for other souls to find peace.

The atmosphere started to turn rather maudlin when two things happened at the same time.

Lex let out a yowl unlike anything I've ever heard from him before and the doorbell rang.

We rushed out of the kitchen looking for Lex. It took a few moments to find him. In an extremely uncharacteristic way, he'd pressed himself under the liquor cart that stood in the room's corner. His eyes were wide and wild and he appeared unable to speak.

I tried to read his mind and only caught snippets of his thoughts.

Don't open the door. Very dangerous. Hide.

The doorbell rang again, and I told Connie what I was getting from Lex.

"We can't ignore it. Whoever it is knows we're in here. This is a business. What do we do?" She asked.

I thought for a moment, then said, "Lex, if you want to leave the room, you can. We have to open the door. We'll be careful, I promise."

Lex crawled out from under the cart. He shook his entire body and blinked slowly. He looked at me and took a deep breath.

"Are you okay?" I asked. "Do you want to leave?"

"No, I will stay. Just promise me you will keep your distance. What's out there is pure evil."

As I asked, "Who?"

Connie asked, "Do you know who it is?"

Before he answered, the front door opened on its own. A very tall man with black hair slicked back from his pointy face, wearing an all black suit, stood in our doorway.

As we stared, open-mouthed and shocked at the intrusion, his gaze landed on each of us. He nodded slightly and smiled. But when his eyes landed on Lex, he stopped smiling.

"Ah, there he is. I've heard tales of you. I

suppose it's nice to meet you, Lex." When he finally tore his eyes from Lex, he zeroed in on Connie. His smile turned my stomach. "My dear, may I come in?"

Worried that she was about to invite a vampire into the house, I jumped into her mind with a loud, "NO!" which thankfully, she picked up on.

"No, I don't believe you can come in, whoever you are. But we can speak on the porch." She motioned for me to follow her outside and for Lex and Sherri to stay inside.

When we closed the front door firmly behind us, the man spoke.

"Forgive me for intruding. I heard you moving around inside and worried that something was wrong after I rang the doorbell several times. I should have known better, though. Of course you are most safe with your daemon." He took a single step backward and bowed. "I am William Black. Perhaps you've heard of me?"

My blood ran cold, and I nodded dumbly. Connie had the presence of mind to extend her hand and shake his as he stood.

"I'm Connie Keyes and this is my business partner, Samantha Collins. How can we help you?"

"Collins, hmm? Changed your last name, did you?"

In point of fact, I changed my last name after the attack in Charleston, but how did he know about it? And why did he care enough to mention it? I didn't answer him and crossed my arms over my chest. I wasn't the one with something to prove here. He came to us.

"Ah, yes, well, I'll get on with it then. No need wasting time. I understand my dear friend Ted Canter is selling his restaurant in order to pay those pesky attorney fees, and I would love to help him out. I'd like to buy The Overlook. I'm prepared to offer twenty-five percent over the asking price." He shifted his gaze to me and added, "I can wire the money immediately. How soon can I sign the papers?"

"I, it," I cleared my throat. "I would...," why was my voice so high? I tried again. "I will need to speak with Mr. Canter first. Last time we talked, he wasn't ready to sell."

"Oh, I suspect you'll find that he's ready to sell now. Especially when he learns what I'm offering."

"Well...," I cleared my throat again. "If you want to leave me a card, I can get back to you after I talk to him."

William Black looked as though he wanted to incinerate me on the spot. And I suspected he could have done so with nothing more than the flick of a finger. Still, I held my ground.

"And you, I suppose, agree with your business partner? We can't do this right now? Make everyone happy?" He put an extra emphasis on the "everyone" part of that.

Connie, love her, pulled herself up taller and agreed with me.

"I believe Ms. Collins has given you her answer. She will take your offer to our client and we will be in touch. Did you want to leave contact information?"

I couldn't read her thoughts, but I could hear her heart racing. She was as terrified as I was by this strange man. Lex was right. Whatever he was, whoever he was, he emanated pure evil and hatred.

Slowly, he reached into a front pocket and pulled out a gold case. He opened it with long, thin fingers tipped with sharp, pointy nails. He flicked a card from the stack and held it out to me.

I took it gingerly and squeaked out that we'd be in touch.

As Connie and I turned to go back inside, he added one more thing.

"Dear Samantha, please get yourself some water and take care of your throat. Sounds like you may be coming down with a cold. And darling Connie, it might be time to see a doctor about that racing heart of yours. Wouldn't want you to have a heart attack now, would we?"

I flung the door open and, without even a

glance back, we both stumbled into the house, then slammed and locked the door behind us.

We were shaking so much that it was difficult to move. Lex took charge and ordered us to sit down immediately.

"Before you pass out," he added under his breath.

He told Sherri to get us both water and a blanket.

When we were settled side by side under a blanket and sipping our drinks, Lex paced.

"I can't believe this. This is so bad. Sherri, I love you, but we are going to need Tawny too. This guy...I just can't believe this. This is so bad."

He went on like that for a few minutes before he stopped in his tracks.

"How did he know you changed your name? Devlin, right? And how did he know about me? And why is he so interested in having the restaurant? I'll bet he killed Franklin. What do you think?"

Before either of us could answer, Sherri piped up.

"Well, I don't know if he killed Franklin. But I'm pretty sure he killed me."

~

I was at a loss for words after that bombshell.

However, Lex didn't have that problem. "No! Really?"

"Yeah, really. I remember him clearly. He came to our house several times. It was kinda like what just happened here. He wanted to buy our house and offered a lot of money for it. But mom and dad said no. Then they started fighting about it. Oh, my gosh! It's all coming back to me now! Yeah! Mom and dad were fighting about it. Mom wanted to sell and get away from him. She was scared. But Dad said he would not be run out of his house and he didn't believe all that stuff about a curse and everything. But I guess Mom was right. I think I'm the result of the curse. And that must be what put Dad over the edge. I remember when he did it. I saw his spirit leave his body. He saw me too, but was swept away too quickly. Oh gosh. Why?"

Sherri's cry was heartbreaking and instinctively Connie and I held out our arms and made room for her on the sofa. She collapsed between us. Lex jumped up as well. The four of us sat huddled on the sofa, holding each other tight. We tried to process not only the tragedy that had befallen Sherri, but the potential tragedy that awaited us.

Still shaken from our meeting with William Black, I struggled to put together the pieces, but Lex's mind was busy at work. He was several steps ahead of me as he solved the puzzle.

"It all points back to him," he said. "William Black is at the root of all of this."

Eventually, I could speak, although my voice was still hoarse and my throat scratchy.

"Why would he kill Sherri? And Franklin? I'm not arguing the point. I don't doubt that he's capable of something like that and probably much more. But I get stuck on why? Why would he murder two people who seem to have nothing in common? What's the connection?"

"I don't know. Call Ted Canter and tell him what happened. See if he has any ideas."

My voice continued to weaken and by the time I had him on the phone, I was completely unable to talk. No words came out at all, and Connie had to take the phone and interpret for me.

Between mouthing words to her and putting phrases into her mind through telepathy, I communicated everything to Ted, who was less than pleased by the offer.

"No. Absolutely not. If William Black wants this place, there's only one reason. He wants to do harm. I don't know what it is about my restaurant, but I'm not turning it over to him. Never."

"We don't blame you, Ted. And we agree. We have one more question, though. Do you remember a family who used to live in the area? The Thompsons? Their daughter, Sherri, was murdered in 1986," Connie paused, waiting for Ted to answer. It took him several beats before he finally answered her.

"I do," he intoned. "Why do you ask?"

Well, that was a loaded question. We hadn't thought this through very well. Connie's eyes went wide as she looked at me, clueless what to say. I shook my head and shrugged.

Connie smiled. "We recently discovered their old house. And you know, since we are a real estate office, we considered renovating and selling, but they demolished the house before the sale went through. We don't know who did it or why. We looked into the house some more and found out about the family. Since you've lived here all your life, we just wondered."

I thought she did spectacularly and covered up her question perfectly. Ted did not.

"You aren't being completely honest with me. That's okay though. You have to be ready to tell me everything. When you are ready, I will listen. For now, though, do you remember I told you about the curses the Black family used to put on people? The things that would happen to them and how their lives would just spin out of control after meeting with that family?"

"Of course."

"Samantha, I think you've been cursed. Losing your voice. When did it start?"

Connie told him it started during our conversation. Then her eyes widened as she related the rest of what he said.

"He said it would be a shame if she lost her voice and that I needed to take care of my heart. What does that mean? Am I going to have a heart attack?"

Lex jumped into her lap and pressed his ear to her chest. He began to purr, and Connie immediately relaxed.

"What's that godawful sound?" Ted asked.

Connie laughed as she stroked Lex's back. "It's our, uh, cat. He is very intuitive and knows when we're upset. He's trying to help me calm down."

"Well, thank goodness for that. Cats are special animals, for sure. Keep him near you, Connie, because if William Black threatened you both, and followed through with Sam, there's nothing to say he won't do the same with you. Please take care. Go to the doctor and get checked out. You may have been cursed. And to answer your other question. Yes, I remember Sherri Thompson and her entire family. It was a tragedy. And it was caused by William Black's curse."

When she hung up, she hugged Lex.

"Well, I guess that answers that," she sighed. She turned to Lex. "Thank you, Lex. You always make me feel better. When we visited Madame, she told me you would be critical in keeping us safe. I wonder if this is what she meant?"

Lex puffed himself up and stood on all fours, his paws making dents in Connie's thighs with his considerable weight. Connie grimaced, but didn't move.

Lex spoke, "I am always critical in protecting you. That will never change. What you saw today will never happen again. He took me by surprise, is all. Now I know."

And with those cryptic words, Lex left us alone with Sherri to figure out how her murder was connected to Franklin's and how we were going to prevent William Black from getting his hands on The Overlook.

CHAPTER 9

The rest of the afternoon passed quietly. Connie made an appointment with her doctor, and I alternated between sucking on cough drops and resting. Sherri was in her room, the sounds of 80s hits thumping through the house.

When the music stopped, the house shook from the thumping of feet on the stairs.

"Guys? Tawny needs to talk to you. We've been working on a way for me to sort of get out of the way."

I tried to speak but a sound like 'ack' came out. When everyone looked at me, I pointed to myself and then my head. Thankfully, Sherri read my mind.

"No, not through telepathy. She wants to actually talk. She thinks she knows what's happening and needs to explain in her words."

"What are you going to do?" Connie asked.

"Well, we've been trying a few different things. I tried to just be small? Sort of shrink out of the way in here. But that didn't work. So, then I tried to do that Joe thing? And attach to something else. And that sorta worked but not really. So, we tried a lot of different things, but unfortunately, that is what worked best."

She pointed to the top of the stairs where Brodie the Beaver sat grinning maniacally. It was so tragic and sad, yet also hysterical, and we all laughed a bit too loud and too long.

"What is it about that dang thing?" Connie muttered when she could finally get enough air to speak.

I spoke into her mind, "I don't know, but I'm glad you kept it."

"Okay, Sherri. How can we help?"

"There's nothing, really," Sherri said. "I need to concentrate? And you guys will help me if I get stuck, right? I don't want to be in that thing forever."

"We'll help you, we promise," Connie said, and I nodded emphatically.

"Okay," Sherri said. "Tawny, here goes!"

I've seen spirits before. I saw Joe when he rescued the souls from Devlin. And I saw the souls themselves. Some were wispy figures, some were orbs of light, and a few, Tawny's grandmother, Joe and Beezel, were in their living forms. But that was brief, and I suspected it only happened because of all the magic and energy in the air that night. I hadn't seen one since, even though, according to Connie, they were still around.

But this time, I saw Sherri as clear as if she were sitting across from me. She was so young. Long brown hair, big green eyes. She even had freckles across the bridge of her nose. She was wearing what she'd been in when she died. Having just returned home from school, she wore acid-washed jeans, Converse high tops, and a pink and yellow t-shirt that hung off of one shoulder.

She didn't look at any of us as she made her way from Tawny's body into the worst looking thing ever made by man. I shuddered, but then remembered that meant we had Tawny!

I turned to her and pulled her into a long hug, quickly joined by Connie. Even Lex smiled at the sight.

"Sherri is great, but we sure have missed you," Connie said as a tear snaked down her cheek.

"Don't even get me started!" Tawny said. "Gosh, it's good to be back. But listen, I don't know how strong Sherri is and how long she can stay in that, um, that thing." She fluttered her hand towards Brodie the Beaver. "So let me get right to it. I've heard everything and I've had talks with Sherri as well. I've also been able to sort of access her memory. It's very weird having her in my mind." She grew silent for a few beats. "But anyway, here's what I think. Have you heard of ley lines?"

Connie and I both nodded while Lex jumped up. "Yes, of course! That's it!"

"We both know about them, but personally, I don't feel Lex's enthusiasm."

"Okay, here's what I think. There must be a ley line between the restaurant and Sherri's old house. Or something like that. A connection that carries energy, power, and William Black wants to tap into it. It explains why he tried to buy that house so long ago and why he had it destroyed before someone else could buy it. And now, why he's so determined to get the restaurant. No one will sell to him, so he puts his curses on the families and makes life miserable until they have no other choice but to leave. Like Sherri's family did."

"It's a really long game though, right? Sherri died forty years ago. And was he trying to get the restaurant all this time?"

"No, but we're assuming those are the only two places he's interested in. If he can amass more points on the lines, it means more energy for him to tap into, and more power. We need to find out what other places he either owns or is trying to buy. That will tell us at least part of the equation."

We all reached for our laptops, and the three of us started tapping. Within a few minutes, I pulled up the realtor's website and found MLS listings that were attached to his name. I turned the screen around and snapped my fingers. Tawny and Connie looked up and nodded.

"Yes, that's it. Exactly. We need a map. Do you have one of those old-fashioned ones?" Tawny asked.

"What do you mean 'old fashioned?'"

"Like it's paper or in a book or something."

Connie stood and mumbled under her breath. "Good grief, she wants an old-fashioned map. Oh, you mean a map. Just a map. They still make these..." and her voice faded as she left the house. I knew where she was going. She was getting the paper map she still kept in her glove box. I would not tell Tawny that, though.

I hated being unable to speak. I missed her so much and wanted to talk.

"I can hear you, you know?" Tawny said smiling.

I keep forgetting, I mentally said as I looked at her and smiled.

"I've missed you too. This won't take much longer. Sherri doesn't want to stay after all. She wants to find her dad."

I can't stand how sad this is, I thought.

Before she said anything else, Connie bustled back into the room, snapping the map open and laying it on the floor in front of us.

Tawny sat down immediately and began connecting the ley lines that we already knew about with the few that I'd found.

I wanted to sit on the floor with her, but I knew once I got down there, I probably wouldn't be able to get back up. Connie had the same issue, so both of us bent over and squinted at the map.

Sure enough, the lines connected and formed the pattern of a star. A star with one particular spot directly in the middle.

"This is where he lives," Lex said, stepping onto the map and pointing with his paw. "Right here, in the middle of it all. If he controls those lines, he controls all that energy. He gets all of that power and who knows what he'll do with it."

~

It's the right thing to do.

"Yeah, but don't you agree this is an exception?"

Sure, but that changes nothing. I still have to let him know.

I was talking to Connie in the car on our way to the doctor. We spoke through telepathy, partly practicing my abilities and partly because we had no other choice. My voice was completely gone.

William Black had sent over another offer that morning. Almost thirty-five percent above the asking price. I had to notify Ted about the offer and desperately hoped he would continue to pass on it.

We had appointments in the same building, but with two different doctors. Mine was fairly simple. I had Connie tell the receptionist that I'd lost my voice. We figured it was a viral infection or something like that, but could they help ease the symptoms at least? Connie's appointment was more serious. She was having some tests for her heart. They wanted to establish a baseline and make sure nothing was currently wrong.

I would finish my appointment before hers was over, which worked out perfectly. I'd use the extra time to text with Ted and follow up about the offer from William Black. It was the right way to do this, and I wasn't worried. Of course, we seriously didn't want him to sell because of the ley lines and we weren't sure what to do about them yet. But Ted didn't want to sell, and I was confident there's no way he'd ever sell to William Black.

About forty-five minutes later, I sat in the waiting room of the heart specialist and texted Ted.

I've lost my voice, so I have to text. Sorry about that.

NP Are you okay?

Yeah. Doc says it's likely a virus. I got a steroid for the inflammation and this stuff to gargle with. It should pass soon.

Good. I really hope that's all it is. Take care of yourself.

Will do. So, I have to tell you there was another offer on the restaurant.

Even though it's not listed? How? Who?

It's another one from William Black. This time 35% over asking.

I stared at the three bubbles as they bounced up and down. Then they went away. I kept staring, waiting for them to come back, but they didn't.

I kept watching, nevertheless, nothing.

Ted? You okay?

Still nothing. Now I was getting worried. I wanted to call, but there was no sound; I mean zero coming from my mouth. I sighed and closed my eyes, resigned to wait for my phone to ding or for Connie to come out. I tried not to worry about both of them, but it was difficult.

Something pulled my attention. I sensed a presence sitting too close. Why did people do that? There were at least five empty chairs in the room and there was no reason to invade my personal space. I opened one eye and tried to see who sat beside me without turning my head.

When I realized who it was, it made sense.

Devlin sat on the edge of his seat. His feet were flat on the floor, his hat balanced on one knee. His hands folded in his lap and his head hung down.

In a low voice that made my stomach flip, he said, "Hello, darlin'. I know you can't speak right now. Are you okay?"

I looked at him with my most stern expression.

He laughed.

"I'll take that as a yes. You are as spunky as ever."

I was going to strangle this guy.

"Listen, I know we haven't always gotten along. There was that whole thing in Charleston and all."

I desperately wanted to say, "You mean when you almost got me killed and instead got my boyfriend to attack me? Then got me in trouble for murder even though it was self-defense? On top of that, you stole our cat? And stole all the innocent souls who were minding their own business so that my best friend's husband had to sacrifice himself to save them all? And in the meantime, you got me to betray my friends and almost destroyed the most important relationships in my life? You mean that little thing?" But, of course, I couldn't say any of that and I wasn't inclined to enter Devlin's mind to put the words there.

"I know, I know. You are still angry with me about all that stuff. But I need you to know this is different, darlin'. This is serious. The man you're dealing with is pure evil. I know, I know," he said when I shot him a look. "You think I'm pure evil. I suppose I get it. You don't like what I do. But there is a reason. I-," he stopped talking.

I looked at him and saw his face soften. What in the world was happening? I held my hand out, palm up, and gestured for him to continue.

"Darlin', um, Samantha, this is hard for an old man to say. But, uh, I was wrong back there. In Charleston. I was on a power trip, I suppose. And I wasn't only going after your people. I had some bad guys trapped. They were spreading some terrible stuff around. I think I got confused and ...," he trailed off.

He made zero sense. Why would he follow us to the doctor's office? What did he want?

I raised an eyebrow and widened my eyes at him. Silently willing him to get on with it and then go away.

Finally, he sighed. "I'm sorry. That's all. I'm

sorry. And I want to help. William Black is going to destroy all of you in that house, and then he'll come after me. We are going to have to work together on this."

I shook my head emphatically, but then Connie emerged. She didn't see Devlin sitting with me and turned immediately to the checkout counter.

"I'll leave. Think about it. I'll be in touch."

And he disappeared in a flash.

Disoriented, I stood and waited while Connie paid her copay. She turned to me and smiled.

"I'm fine. In fact, everything is great. How about you?"

I smiled and hugged her. I showed her my prescription and a note I'd written explaining what the doctor said.

"Thank goodness. William Black is full of it. Harmless old creep," she muttered.

I grabbed her arm and shook my head. When I had her attention, I put my entire conversation with Devlin into her mind. I also told her how Ted stopped texting the second I mentioned William Black's second offer.

"So not harmless then."

I shook my head.

"Let's go see Ted," she suggested.

I nodded agreement. But first, we'd go home and pick up Lex. After what Devlin said, no way was I going anywhere else without him.

~

Tawny and Sherri wanted to go with us to the restaurant, especially after Connie told them what Devlin had said to me. No one wanted Sherri to go. It was too dangerous. But if we wanted Tawny there, and really, we needed Tawny there; we had to have Sherri as well.

While we were at our appointments, Sherri practiced moving between Tawny and Brodie and was getting very good at it. Still, no one felt comfortable with the idea of leaving her alone in the house, stuck in Brodie.

So yet again, we hauled the thing to the car and set him up in the backseat, buckled in and ready for action.

"How is it in there?" Connie asked.

"It's weird," Sherri admitted. "Sort of lonely, but in a comforting way. I don't have to work at anything. I can just relax and know nothing is going to bother me. Ya' know?"

We didn't, but we nodded agreeably. It was good that she felt that way. And as a special perk, we discovered I could communicate telepathically with her. Even when she was in Brodie. This gave me access to Tawny and Sherri at the same time.

We pulled into the restaurant's parking lot. I drove while Lex sat on Connie's lap, Tawny and Sherri sat in the backseat with Brodie. The parking lot was deserted, even though it was late afternoon.

"Where is everyone?" Connie asked.

I shrugged.

"Shouldn't they be setting up? For dinner?" Sherri asked.

Lex mumbled, "Yeah. They should. Let me out. You all stay here."

I objected, sending my thoughts to Lex at the same time Connie spoke up, saying much the same thing.

Lex paused. "You two. Knock it off. Let me do my job. Open the door."

Connie did as commanded. We'd never seen Lex so determined and, well, cranky. We shared a mutual look of concern. Then the car grew quiet. Everyone was lost in their own thoughts.

I did a little snooping, but not much. Connie was easy. I didn't have to enter her mind to know what she was thinking. It was much the same as me. She was worried about Lex, worried about Ted, worried about Sherri, and wondering what Devlin was up to and if we could trust him - we couldn't. She also wondered how this all fit together with William Black and the ley lines.

Tawny thought similar thoughts, although she focused more on strategy with the ley lines. While

Sherri had been riding along in her mind, she wasn't able to reach out to her mother, Orenda. But now, things were back to normal, and she happily strategized with her in their old manner. Orenda knew a lot more about William Black's potential power and how he could harness the ley lines.

Sherri's thoughts were heartbreaking. Alone in Brodie the Beaver, without Tawny's thoughts overlapping her own, she was spiraling. Her mind jumped everywhere but kept ending up on Missy, Ted's employee. Of all the things going on right now, Sherri was most worried about that young woman's safety.

I backed out of her mind slowly and carefully and turned my thoughts back to Lex.

What are you seeing?

It feels strange here, Sam. It's not right. Something is very wrong. I'd love it if you all would leave.

No, Lex, that's not happening.

"What's he saying?" Connie whispered.

"He says it feels strange, and he wants us to leave," I whispered back.

Then it hit me.

The car erupted in cheers and exclamations as the reality of what happened set in.

"You have your voice back!"

"What happened?"

"How? Do you feel okay?"

When everyone settled, I experimented a little.

“Yes,” I began slowly. “I feel fine. And I don’t know what happened. It just changed.”

Suddenly, I heard Lex loud and clear.

What’s going on there? Did something happen? Are you okay?

I turned to the group.

“Lex is asking about us. Hold on.”

I told him I’d gotten my voice back and asked about him.

If you refuse to leave, then you need to get in here now. Be careful and be quiet. And leave Sherri in the car.

CHAPTER 10

We prepared for a showdown. Tawny explained that the restaurant sat on a junction in the ley lines. It was a place of increased energy, therefore making it extremely important that William Black did not get his hands on it.

"Remember the markings in the basement of Sherri's house? Orenda thinks there's something like that here and if he taps into that energy, he'll only get stronger," she said. "Orenda said his family has been searching the world for junctions and slowly amassing great powers. The reason he could affect your voice is that our own house is on a line. The same one Sherri's house is on. When he isn't in close contact with an actual ley line, his power diminishes. But the catch is, owning and having constant access to a junction, like the restaurant, allows him to sort of fill the tanks. So he can travel and move around but carry the power with him."

"Bottom line, we need to keep him as far from this place as we can," Connie said.

"Exactly."

Armed with our new information but no actual plan, we followed Lex's directions and made our way into the storeroom in the back of the restaurant.

The room was colder than normal and the lights were dim. It felt heavy and uncomfortable. I immediately saw Ted sitting at a table with his head in his hands. He didn't look up when we came in. Missy stood in a corner with her arms crossed over her chest. She stared at the floor, occasionally stomping her foot and grumbling to herself.

Connie caught my eye and nodded to her side, indicating that Franklin's ghost was also there.

But what made my blood run cold was the image of William Black. He leaned against the far wall, tucked away into the shadows where he could barely be seen. His eyes glowed an otherworldly bright green, and tiny sparks flew from his fingertips. He watched the sparks with interest and didn't seem to notice or care that we'd arrived.

Lex spoke into my mind.

They don't know we're here. All of them are in some sort of trance or something.

I told Connie and Tawny what he said, and they replied that Franklin said the same thing and had been watching them for a while now.

Connie gestured towards the door with her head, and Tawny, Lex, and I followed.

Once we moved away from the strange room, we spoke freely.

Lex, as usual, went first.

"When I got here, that's how I found them. I do not know what's going on. Franklin, do you?"

Connie and Tawny suddenly burst into laughter, and even Lex smiled. With all the magic and strangeness, no one thought about poor Franklin, recently deceased, who had never seen a talking cat.

"He just went poof!" Tawny giggled.

I wished I'd seen it for myself. I needed a good laugh to break the tension. Watching my friends laugh helped though, and I was happy they could find some humor in the situation.

"Okay, Franklin, sorry about that. I'm glad you're back," Connie said. Then she introduced everyone quickly. "This is Tawny. This is Sam, you saw her that day in the bathroom. Unfortunately she still can't see you though."

I waved a hand in the general direction, feeling like an idiot.

Connie continued. "And this is Lex. He's a daemon in the form of a cat. Oh, and Sherri is also a lost spirit, but she is waiting in the car for us."

"Um, guys?" Lex whispered. He pointed to the door, then quickly ducked out of sight.

Tyler walked in carrying Brodie the Beaver.

He looked at us, then walked by, saying, "Yeah, you left something in your car. Bill asked me to get it on my way in. Come on everyone. We got stuff to settle."

We had no choice but to follow him. He had Sherri.

I tapped into her mind and heard her frantic questions.

What's happening? Where am I? Are you guys there?

I explained quickly and calmly and reminded her to be quiet. We wanted her hidden as much as possible.

Then I shifted my thoughts to Lex. He'd closed his mind to me and I had no idea what he was thinking.

Once in the storeroom, Tyler directed us to the table where Ted sat. He shot a hard look at Missy, who still stared at the floor. Apparently satisfied that he had everyone positioned where he wanted us to be, he approached William Black.

I barely heard Connie whisper, "Do you know what's happening?"

I knew she asked Franklin and waited for her

signal before entering her mind for the details. When she had the story, she nodded slightly, and I heard what Franklin told her.

"William Black arrived and Ted tried to run him off. Ted has court tomorrow and is super stressed out. He closed the restaurant to prepare, but had Missy come in to help a bit. Just after his lawyer left, William arrived. Franklin thinks he was texting with you when that happened."

I nodded.

"Well, that gave Ted enough warning that he knew why William came here, and he sent Missy to hide in the storeroom. Unfortunately, that's exactly where William wanted to go. He said something about where the power felt the strongest. Franklin said he suspects William is trying to keep Ted away from court tomorrow. If he didn't show up, he'd be in even more trouble and then William could force the sale."

What's going on then? What's happening now?

I sent my question to everyone who could hear me.

Tawny leaned in close. "I don't think they can hear us. I think he's tapping into the ley lines' powers. Remember? The restaurant is on a junction. It must be right below this room. He has to own the property to get the full benefit, though. It looks like he's practicing."

I wanted to keep Brodie in my sights, and I was

also worried about Missy and Ted. They were in some sort of trance. Added to that, I didn't know where Lex was or what he was up to, and all the interpretations I was doing plus the overall heaviness of the room was exhausting me. I understood why Ted had his head on the table. It would be nice to close my eyes and lay my head down.

Connie and Tawny obviously had the same feelings. I saw both of them nodding off, heads dropping, only to be jerked up again. They tried to fight it but had no more success than I did.

If I had to guess one thing that would awaken all of us, I never in a million years would have guessed what happened next.

A flash of grey and white shot into the room and jumped onto the table. Lex stood on his back legs, looking even more like a dignified politician in a tuxedo. His features evolved before us as his paws turned into hands and his face became more human-like. His eyes glowed bright green and even his body seemed to shimmer. He grew at least a foot taller and his ears lay flat against his head.

Tawny found her voice. "Lex! What's happening?"

"I am doing what I was created for. This is my purpose. Do not argue with me. Follow my directions completely. Do not challenge me."

No one dared to talk back. We had no other

directions to follow, and by all means, we certainly were not in a position to challenge him.

"Slowly get up and leave this room. Ignore that idiot Tyler, no matter what he says or does. Take Sherri, Missy, and Ted with you. And when Devlin comes, let him through. Don't stop him."

That shook all of us out of our stupor.

"Devlin?" Connie asked.

Lex didn't answer her. He looked right through her. Then turned his full attention on William Black.

~

"Now what?" I asked.

No one had an answer. Apparently Devlin would be here soon. Devlin, whose sole purpose in life up to this point, had been to doggedly and effectively steal the souls of those we loved. And he was coming here. Where Franklin and Sherri were vulnerable and unprepared.

And to make it worse, a daemon commanded us to allow it to happen.

Missy and Ted were like zombies, but able to move, at least. I reached out to Sherri, still tucked away inside Brodie. She insisted she was okay, but her voice shook.

Connie checked her phone. "How long do we wait?"

"And what's Tyler doing in there?"

The response to our questions came quickly when a panicked Tyler ran frantically through the room. His hair was now bright white and his face was dull and pale. He bounced off of tables and slammed into chairs as he blindly clawed his way through the dining area. When he reached the front door, he ripped it open and tumbled across the porch and down the steps. The last we saw of him was flashes of white through the trees that lined the property.

It was funny, really. And in any other circumstance, we all would have laughed.

"I think we got our answer," Connie deadpanned.

With wry grins on our faces and knots in our stomachs, the three of us stayed where Lex had ordered us. We desperately wanted to know what was happening in the other room, but there was no way we could. Tawny chewed her lower lip. Connie picked at her fingernails. I paced. It felt like forever, but after only ten minutes, things started happening quickly.

First Devlin arrived. He had his evil box with him tucked up under his arm. I remembered holding a box very much like that one and smashing it with all my might. That was the night I redeemed myself with my friends and released the souls of Tawny's grandmother, Beezel, and other innocents. It was also the night Connie lost Joe again. Seeing that box brought up a lot of feelings for me and I steadfastly avoided Connie's mind. I could only imagine what it brought up for her, and I didn't want to feel that pain again.

Devlin scanned the room, then said, "Come along, ladies. We have work to do. Let's help your little kitty cat put an end to this."

Taking orders from a talking cat was one thing. But we respected and loved Lex, so it was okay. However, the prospect of taking orders from Devlin gave us pause. I could feel the objections and hesitation from everyone in the room. Hesitation turned to outright refusal as we balked at the command.

Devlin looked at each of us and shrugged. Then he marched into the storeroom.

We had no choice. If we wanted to know what was happening, we had to follow.

None of us were prepared for what we saw.

William Black and Lex faced each other, locked in some sort of electrical current. Neither of them moved, but I didn't think they could have if they'd wanted to.

None of it bothered Devlin, and he leaped into action.

"We need to get Ted and Missy out of the way. Tawny, put them over there in case we need them. Oh, and by the way, nice to have you back."

I saw Tawny wretch a bit from the corner of my eye, but she nodded and immediately went to work shepherding the two where Devlin pointed.

"I know there's a ghost here. Is it the man they are accusing Ted of killing? What's his name? Franklin?" He asked me.

I nodded. "Yes, I can't see him, but they said he's here."

"Franklin, my man. I need you over here, by this box. When I open it, I need you to communicate with the souls who come out. Here's what you tell them."

"No!" My voice was louder than I intended and Devlin stopped to look at me. "No, Franklin, stay away. Far away." I said into empty space, hoping Franklin had heard me.

Devlin grabbed my arm and pulled me close. "You have got to trust me. Your kitty cat does and called me here. See him over there? Getting electrocuted? You want that? Stop interfering and help instead."

My blood boiled. There were so many things I wanted to say. Terrible memories and hateful thoughts flew through my mind. Most of them involved Devlin's painful demise. But through the rage that consumed me, I heard Sherri's voice, begging me to be patient. Reminding me what was at stake.

I nodded curtly and stepped aside. Connie reached out for my hand and pulled me close to her.

"Franklin is listening to Devlin. It'll be okay," she whispered and gave my hand a quick squeeze.

"I can't hold him any longer," Lex yelled. "It's now or never. He's too strong for me."

Immediately, Devlin smashed the box.

A thick, luminescent mist poured out like water from a jug. As it cascaded to the floor, tiny tendrils seemed to separate from the mass. I shivered as the temperature in the room dropped.

"Oh my god! NO!" Connie screamed.

CHAPTER 11

For the last few years, I've lived with people who could see ghosts and communicate with them. I've even lived with those very ghosts. Yet I only saw them for myself twice. At least until now.

For the third time in my life, I saw what my friends saw. My stomach flipped when the form of Sherri appeared in the mist. Was this some elaborate plan from Devlin to capture not just Franklin, but also Sherri?

"We have to stop him," I said.

"Sherri! No!" Connie and Tawny yelled at the same time.

The three of us moved towards the box and Sherri, but we didn't make it very far.

The connection between Lex and William Black suddenly failed. Lex shot towards William, who was moving his hands in a circle in front of his body. As his hands circled, a ball of electricity and energy grew between his fingers. It became bigger and brighter quickly.

Shadows formed within the mist, still coming from the box. They drifted past Franklin, who stood his ground in the center of it all. He spoke rapidly and animatedly as fleeting human features emerged like a mirage and then disappeared again.

Sherri stood beside him. Pointing and directing some in one direction and others in another direction.

Soon, the mist encompassed William, yet he continued to wield his power. He threw off several figures while others dissipated and then reformed. They all kept going, but William wasn't weakening.

Once we understood what was happening, and we knew Sherri was safe, we joined in trying to help the spirts understand the danger. We all needed some way to defend ourselves, but no matter what we said or did, the ball of energy William held continued to grow bigger and brighter.

Lex was exhausted, but kept fighting. He was trying to connect to the energy like he had before, but this time he just kept getting shocked.

"STOP IT NOW!"

The voice was so loud it shook the walls. Everyone, including the spirits, Devlin, and Lex, stopped in their tracks. William's eyes widened, and he looked at the source of the voice.

It was Missy. Floating at least a foot from the ground, her hair flew in all directions, glowing gold and bright. She looked like an angel, but a furious one. Like a parent scolding a little child, she shot towards William and simply held her hand out.

"No, it's mine," he said, being the eternally petulant child.

She continued to float in front of him, hand out, palm up.

"Noooo," he wailed.

"Give it," she said.

William Black let out a whimper. He handed over the ball of energy and collapsed to the floor.

Within seconds, the room returned to a normal temperature, and the heaviness lifted. We heard police sirens in the distance and, as if on cue, Lex disappeared. He never wanted to be around when the police were asking questions.

Missy reverted to her normal form and quietly sank into the background. She seemed content to watch. She had completed her role.

The surrounding spirits drifted away slowly. We scanned the room for familiar faces, wanting assurance that all were safe and not somehow harmed or trapped by Devlin.

We saw Franklin first. He waved to us and then blew a kiss to Connie as his spirit drifted upwards.

Devlin was preparing to avoid the police as well, but before he ran, he gently touched my arm and pointed to a corner of the storeroom.

"Ladies, look."

As the mist cleared, we could see Tawny and Sherri. They were talking to a man. Sherri was grinning and holding his hand. Then she hugged Tawny and turned back towards the man, who wrapped his arms around her with fierce protectiveness.

The two of them drifted upwards. Then she caught sight of Connie and me. She waved her arms and pointed to the man beside her.

"My dad!" she said.

CHAPTER 12

Devlin must have trapped her father with the other spirits in his box. I turned to ask him when he did that, but he'd already disappeared.

This left the three of us, Ted, Missy, and a quivering and quaking William Black, to explain to the police what had happened.

Of course, they had many questions, mostly for Ted, but they also wanted to know why we were there. It was easy enough to explain ourselves. We were Ted's friends, and also helping him with the sale of his restaurant. We left William Black to explain his presence on his own.

I felt a great relief to see him sitting in the back of the cruiser. His long face drawn even more in defeat. Ted explained William had refused to leave. Then I disclosed how he was trying to force Ted into selling the restaurant and had tried to intimidate us. They decided it was worth asking him a few more questions.

They advised Ted to call his attorney and come to the station later that day, too. Unfortunately, they had more questions for him as well.

"I'm not worried," he told us. "I think after everything that happened here, this could be enough to provide reasonable doubt."

"Let us know if we can help at all," Connie added. "Anything we can do, we are here for you."

"Thank you all," he said. Then his gaze shifted. "Missy? Are you okay?"

Missy had followed the group around the restaurant after the police arrived. She found an out of the way spot where she was close yet discreet and listened to everything.

When Ted addressed her, she lifted her head and smiled slightly.

"All good," she said.

"You sure did surprise us all in there," he said. "What happened?"

We held our breath, waiting to hear of Missy's magical abilities, her hidden talents, her special skills.

Instead of an elaborate explanation, though, she simply said, "Nothing. Thanks for the ghosts. They helped a lot." Then she tossed her marble into the air, caught it and dramatically placed it into her pocket. "This is mine," she said with the smallest hint of a smile. Then she floated into the kitchen, leaving us with even more questions.

"What in the world?"

Ted shook his head. "I don't know. I've always known she had a special connection with this place and I've always believed she needed to be here no matter what. Honestly, though, I'm not asking any more questions. I'm just glad she's on my side, you know?"

We did.

Unfortunately, they didn't hold William Black for long. They released him the next day during what was the first day of Ted's trial.

We attended the trial every day we could, and I was even called as a witness to explain how persistent William Black was that Ted sell the restaurant to him. They couldn't indict William Black for Franklin's murder. But, considering everything that happened, it was enough to plant reasonable doubt in the minds of the jurors. They found Ted innocent.

William Black remained free, and that made all of us nervous.

Lex reminded us he was always there. "Plus, don't forget about Missy. She controls that spot where the junction is. I don't see anyone taking that away from her, do you?"

Devlin had all but disappeared. A part of me wanted to wring his neck for trapping Sherri's father, but if he hadn't, who knows what would have happened that day. I have a sort of image in my mind of Devlin running through a field with a giant net, trying to catch not butterflies, but spirits. An evil grin on his face as he tucks them away in his little box. I hoped that wasn't happening, but there was no way to tell. Devlin would show up again. There was no doubt in my mind. I sure wasn't in any hurry to see him, though.

The lot where Sherri's house had stood was eventually cleared, and Tawny surprised us one day with her announcement.

"I've decided to rebuild on the lot. A small bungalow for myself. I love you guys, but I want to live in my own place. I'll still be close, okay?"

"You don't have to ask permission!" Connie laughed. "You're an adult."

Tawny laughed as well. "After having Sherri's thoughts in my head for so long, a part of me feels like a teenager again. I keep forgetting that I'm not. Although that experience made me realize how much I still want to do with my life and living on my own is one of those things. I want my own house."

"I think it's very fitting that you live there. It's a

terrific memorial of what you've been through and a great way to honor Sherri and her family. It also locks down another house on the ley line," I added wryly.

"I don't think we'll have too many problems with that," Connie said. "Like Lex mentioned, we have his protection, and Missy isn't giving up that marble. That power she has is plenty to keep that junction safe."

"Still, it just seemed too easy, you know?" I asked.

"I do," Connie agreed.

Nonetheless, we put our faith in Missy and believed that she had it under control. Whatever that meant for her.

With a collective sigh of relief that things were finally returning to normal, we decided to watch *The Breakfast Club* in honor of our dear friend, Sherri. When Brian began reading the essay and the closing song rang out, we couldn't help but dance around the room, promising Sherri that we most certainly would not be forgetting about her... ever.

CHAPTER 13

"What do you want to drink?" Connie called out to the backyard.

It was one of the last fall days we would have before winter set in with a vengeance. The weather was breezy, as usual, but the sun shined bright. I wore a soft sweatshirt and sweatpants with a fuzzy blanket over my shoulders. I sat on the porch watching college football.

"I don't know. Something good," I called back.

Tawny was busy decorating her new house and planned to stop by later that afternoon. For now, Connie and I were fully enjoying the prospect of a long, lazy weekend ahead of us. No plans, no responsibilities.

"Oh! I know!" I heard her exclaim. I started to ask what she knew, but thought better of it. I didn't really care. I put my feet up and squinted at the screen. The official missed it again. The NCAA really needed to do something about the incompetence of their officials. There were too many missed or bad calls affecting the outcomes of games this season. It was frustrating.

I was about to let the TV have an earful of my opinions when Connie arrived with a tray of snacks and two tall glasses of something fizzy.

"Ginger collins," she smiled. "The easiest thing ever to make and the best thing to drink on a day like this."

I didn't ask, but she told me the ingredients, anyway.

"So, it's one and a half ounces of London Dry Gin, three quarters ounce of Domaine de Canton, that's that ginger liqueur that's so good, and half ounce of lemon juice. You shake that with ice and then strain it into the glass and top with about three ounces of club soda. Oh! And the lemon wedge, I forgot those. Hold on!"

I heard her phone ring while she was in the kitchen. I waited a hot minute then decided I didn't need to wait for the garnish in order to enjoy my drink. It was fabulous.

By the time she returned, I'd eaten several crackers and cheese slices, drank half my ginger collins, and the officials had missed another holding. But Connie looked upset.

"What's wrong?"

“That was Madame,” she hesitated.

“Is she okay? Does she need something?”

“She’s insisting that we host a writer’s retreat. Here. It’s for a friend of hers and she said this place is perfect for them. I tried to explain to her we don’t really do that anymore, but she wouldn’t listen.”

“Well, we do sort of owe her. I mean, she’s gotten us out of a few jams over the years. It won’t hurt anything. We’ll cater it. There’s plenty of room and I can bunk with you if we need my room. Plus a bunch of writers. It could be fun.”

Connie didn’t seem convinced and was even less enthusiastic when the mentor of the writer’s group called to confirm not even ten minutes later. She put her on speaker.

“I will need silence for the retreat. The only voice to be heard should be mine. I have four authors who are all blocked, and I am determined that they will follow my instructions to the letter. If they do exactly as I say when I say it, I know they will start writing again. Even if it kills me, I will have them writing within the weekend. Mark my words...even if it kills me.”

Of course, you know good and well it kills her! But how? And why? And who? Get your copy of

Mediums and Margaritas, Book 2 in the *Mystic on the Rocks* series and tune in today!

~

If you enjoyed reading ***Hot Flashes and Highballs***, please consider leaving a review or a star rating. This is the best way to let others know if they might like this book as well. Thank you!

~

I'd love to stay in touch! **Click here to join my monthly newsletter for updates, sneak peeks, and specials!**

ALSO BY LYNN M. STOUT

Scan the QR code above to discover more books by Lynn M. Stout and to join my monthly newsletter.

Find more books by Lynn M. Stout and other cozy mystery authors at the independent book store dedicated to cozy mystery readers! **Visit Mystic Valley Press by scanning the code above.**

Made in the USA
Las Vegas, NV
06 July 2025

24508859R00090